POKÉMON™

BLACK AND WHITE

VOL.7

Story by **HIDENORI KUSAKA**
Art by **SATOSHI YAMAMOTO**

Pokémon Black and White
Volume 7
VIZ Kids Edition

Story by HIDENORI KUSAKA
Art by SATOSHI YAMAMOTO

English Adaptation / Annette Roman
Translation / Tetsuichiro Miyaki
Touch-up & Lettering / Susan Daigle-Leach
Design / Fawn Lau
Cover Colorist / Chii (Chelsea) Maene
Editor / Annette Roman

Printed in the U.S.A.

Published by VIZ Media, LLC
P.O. Box 77010
San Francisco, CA 94107

10 9 8 7 6 5 4 3 2 1
First printing, May 2012

www.vizkids.com

www.viz.com

PARENTAL ADVISORY
POKÉMON ADVENTURES
is rated A and is suitable
for readers of all ages.
ratings.viz.com

Pokémon

BLACK AND WHITE

VOL.7

THE STORY THUS FAR!

Pokémon Trainer Black is exploring the mysterious Unova Region with his brand-new Pokédex. Pokémon Trainer White runs a thriving talent agency for performing Pokémon. Now she has hired Black as her assistant. Meanwhile, Team Plasma is plotting to separate Pokémon from their beloved humans...!

BLACK'S dream is to win the Pokémon League!

WHITE'S dream is to make her Tepig Gigi a star!

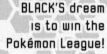

Black's Munna, MUSHA, helps him think clearly by temporarily "eating" his dream.

White's Tepig, GIGI, and Black's Pignite, NITE, get along like peanut butter and jelly!

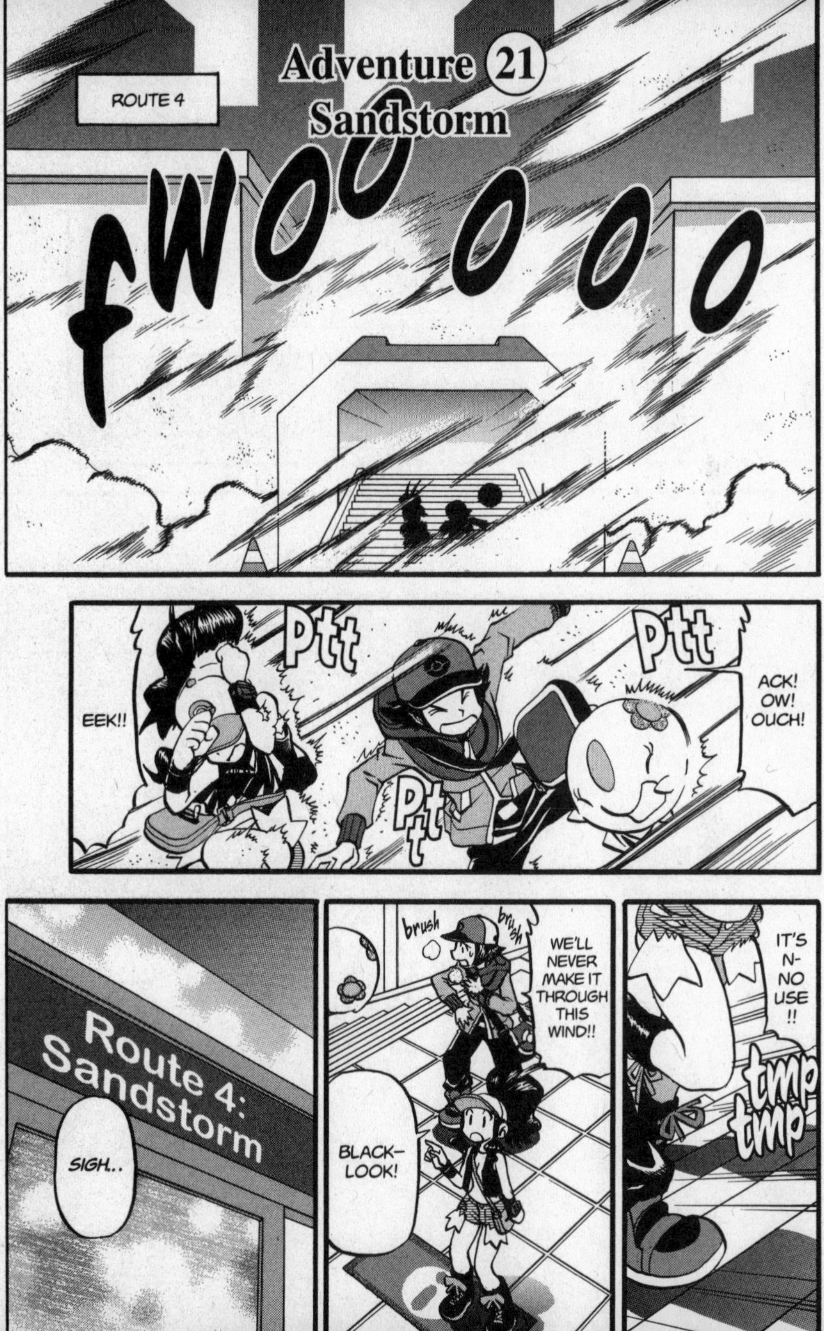
Adventure 21
Sandstorm
ROUTE 4
FWOOOOOO
EEK!!
Ptt
Ptt
Ptt
ACK! OW! OUCH!
Route 4: Sandstorm
SIGH..
brush
brush
WE'LL NEVER MAKE IT THROUGH THIS WIND!!
BLACK— LOOK!
IT'S N-NO USE!!
tmp
tmp

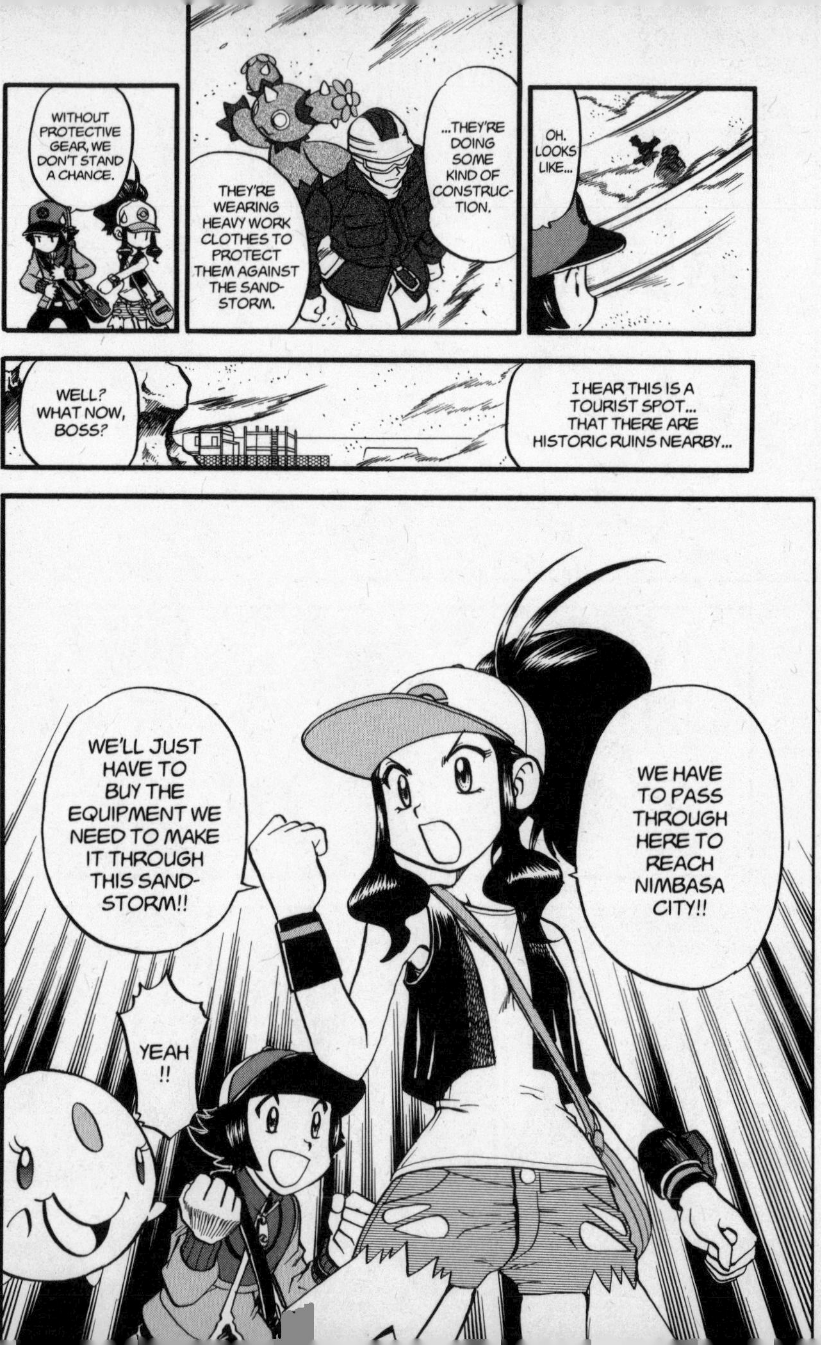
OH. LOOKS LIKE...
...THEY'RE DOING SOME KIND OF CONSTRUCTION.
THEY'RE WEARING HEAVY WORK CLOTHES TO PROTECT THEM AGAINST THE SANDSTORM.
WITHOUT PROTECTIVE GEAR, WE DON'T STAND A CHANCE.
I HEAR THIS IS A TOURIST SPOT... THAT THERE ARE HISTORIC RUINS NEARBY...
WELL? WHAT NOW, BOSS?
WE HAVE TO PASS THROUGH HERE TO REACH NIMBASA CITY!!
WE'LL JUST HAVE TO BUY THE EQUIPMENT WE NEED TO MAKE IT THROUGH THIS SANDSTORM!!
YEAH !!

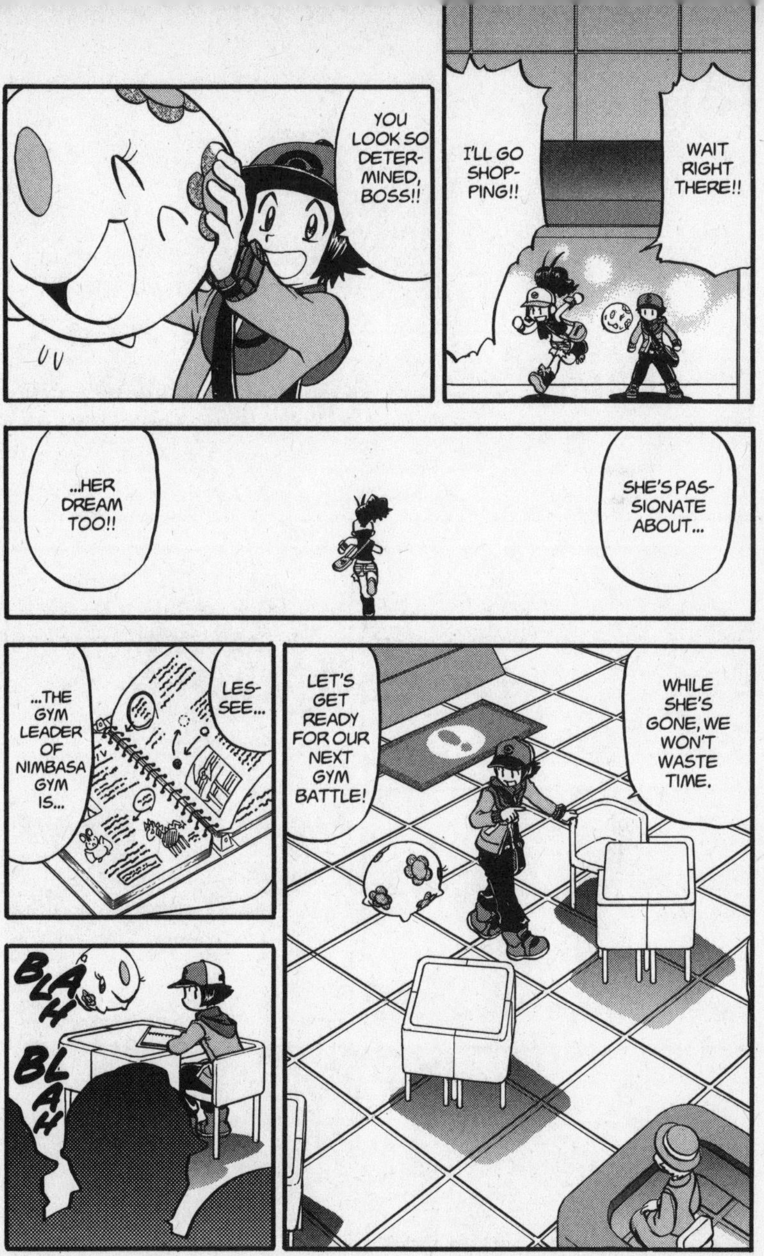
WAIT RIGHT THERE!!
I'LL GO SHOPPING!!
YOU LOOK SO DETERMINED, BOSS!!
SHE'S PASSIONATE ABOUT...
...HER DREAM TOO!!
WHILE SHE'S GONE, WE WON'T WASTE TIME.
LET'S GET READY FOR OUR NEXT GYM BATTLE!
LES-SEE...
...THE GYM LEADER OF NIMBASA GYM IS...
BLAH BLAH BLAH

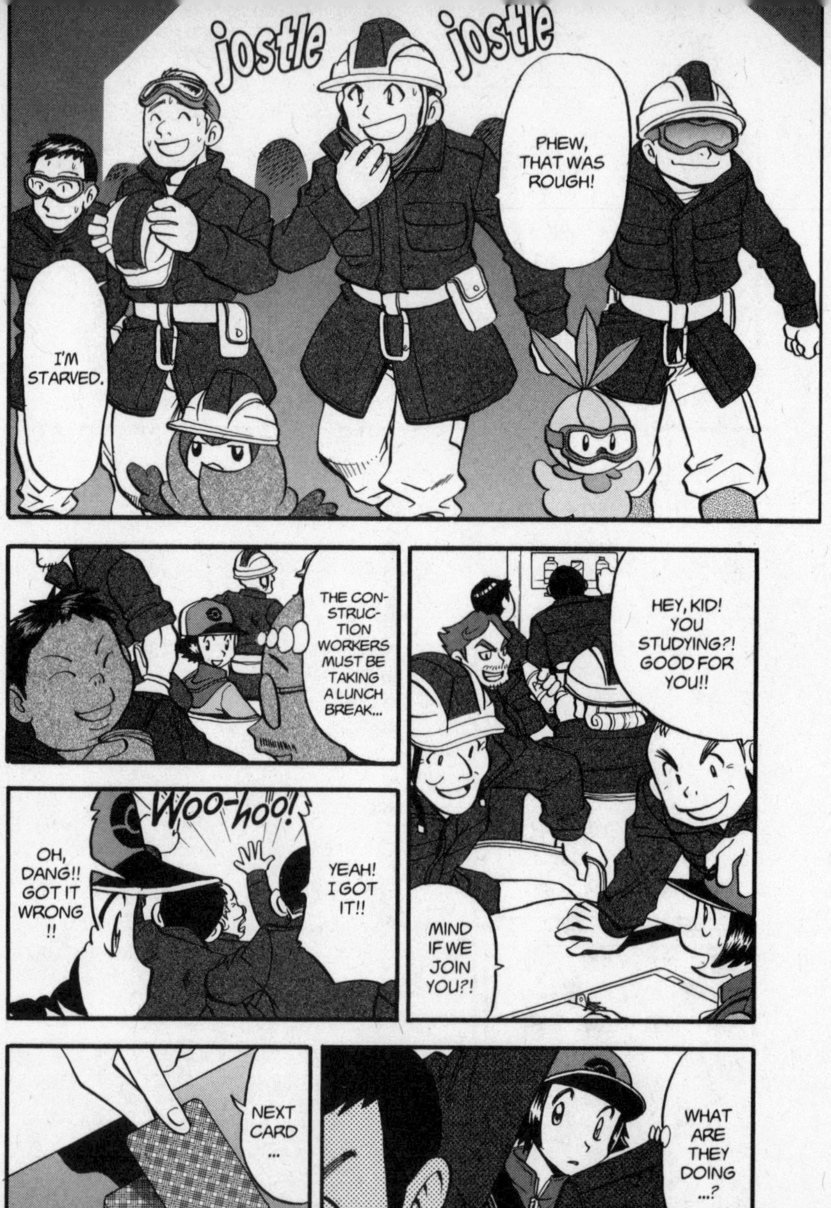
jostle jostle
PHEW, THAT WAS ROUGH!
I'M STARVED.
THE CONSTRUCTION WORKERS MUST BE TAKING A LUNCH BREAK...
HEY, KID! YOU STUDYING?! GOOD FOR YOU!!
MIND IF WE JOIN YOU?!
Woo-hoo!
YEAH! I GOT IT!!
OH, DANG!! GOT IT WRONG!!
NEXT CARD...
WHAT ARE THEY DOING...?

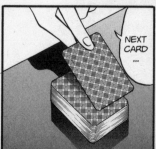

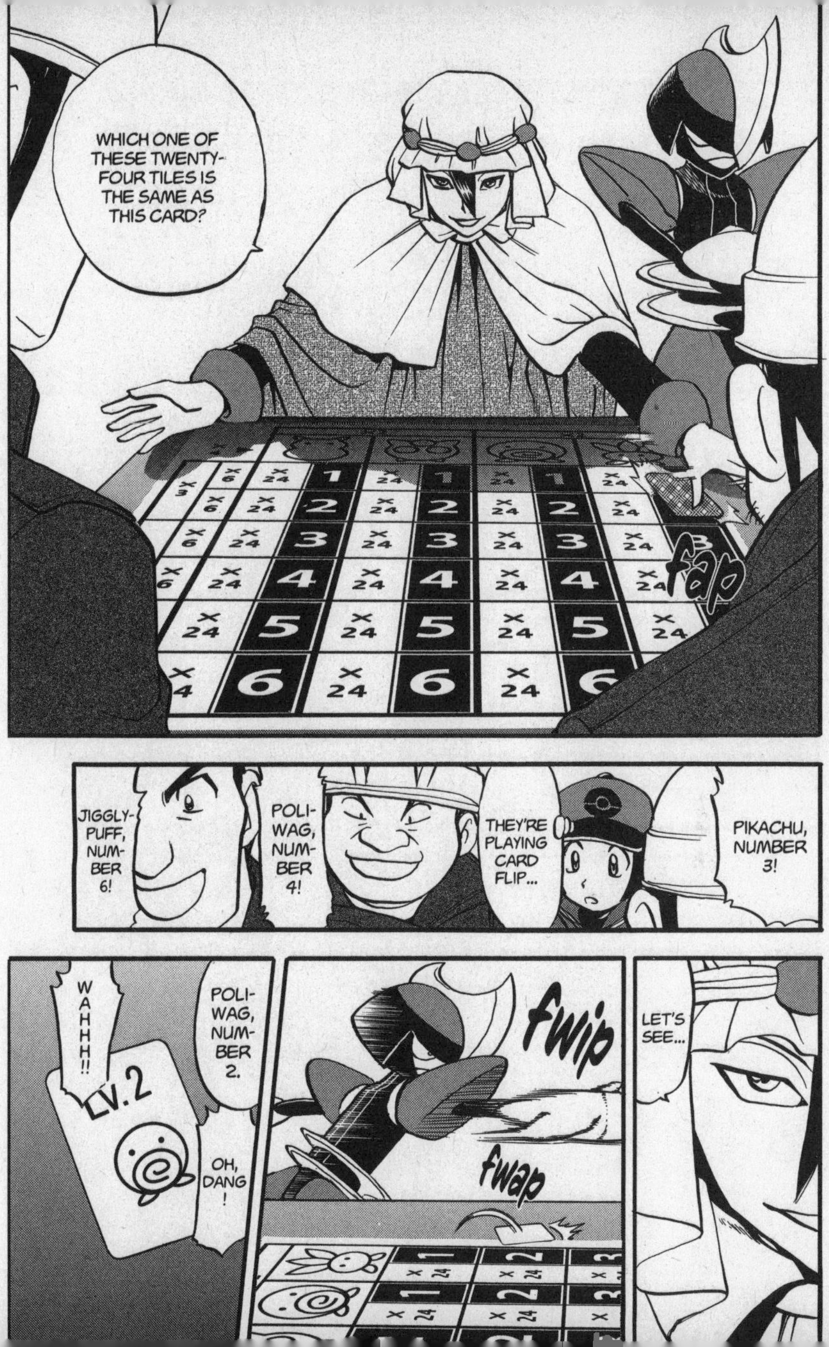
WHICH ONE OF THESE TWENTY-FOUR TILES IS THE SAME AS THIS CARD?
fap
JIGGLYPUFF, NUMBER 6!
POLIWAG, NUMBER 4!
THEY'RE PLAYING CARD FLIP...
PIKACHU, NUMBER 3!
WAHHH!!
LV. 2
POLIWAG, NUMBER 2.
OH, DANG!
fwip
fwap
LET'S SEE...

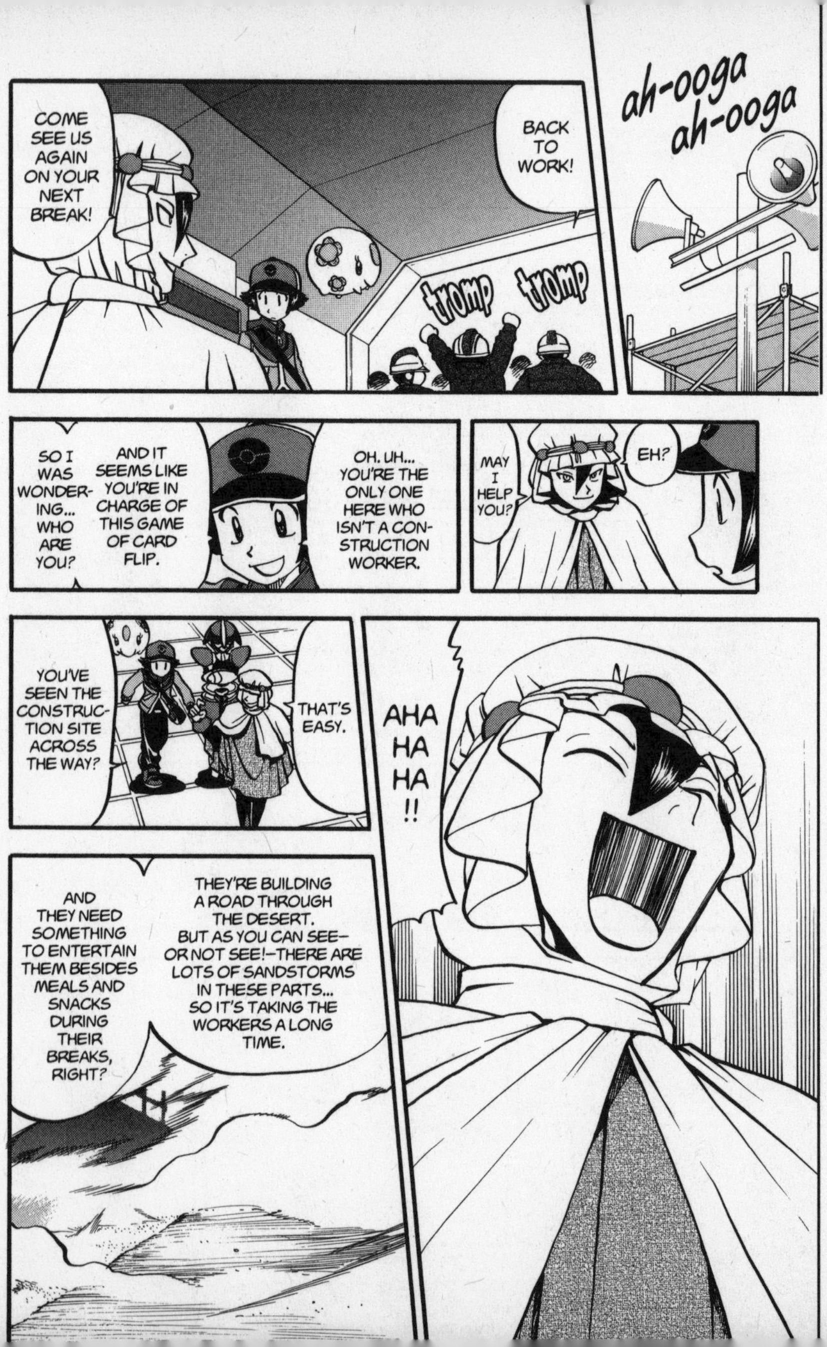

ah-ooga
ah-ooga
BACK TO WORK!
tromp tromp
COME SEE US AGAIN ON YOUR NEXT BREAK!
EH?
MAY I HELP YOU?
OH. UH... YOU'RE THE ONLY ONE HERE WHO ISN'T A CONSTRUCTION WORKER.
AND IT SEEMS LIKE YOU'RE IN CHARGE OF THIS GAME OF CARD FLIP.
SO I WAS WONDERING... WHO ARE YOU?
AHA HA HA !!
THAT'S EASY.
YOU'VE SEEN THE CONSTRUCTION SITE ACROSS THE WAY?
THEY'RE BUILDING A ROAD THROUGH THE DESERT. BUT AS YOU CAN SEE— OR NOT SEE!—THERE ARE LOTS OF SANDSTORMS IN THESE PARTS... SO IT'S TAKING THE WORKERS A LONG TIME.
AND THEY NEED SOMETHING TO ENTERTAIN THEM BESIDES MEALS AND SNACKS DURING THEIR BREAKS, RIGHT?

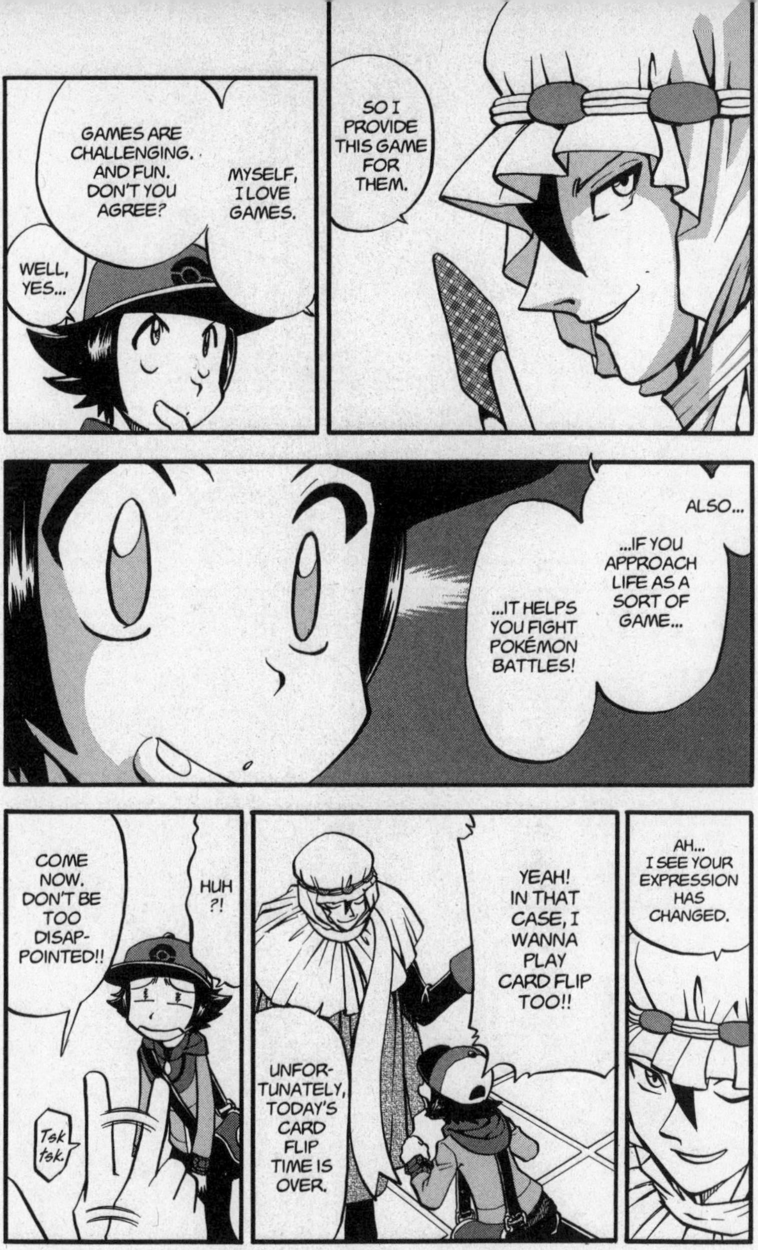
SO I PROVIDE THIS GAME FOR THEM.
MYSELF, I LOVE GAMES.
GAMES ARE CHALLENGING. AND FUN. DON'T YOU AGREE?
WELL, YES...
ALSO...
...IF YOU APPROACH LIFE AS A SORT OF GAME...
...IT HELPS YOU FIGHT POKÉMON BATTLES!
AH... I SEE YOUR EXPRESSION HAS CHANGED.
YEAH! IN THAT CASE, I WANNA PLAY CARD FLIP TOO!!
UNFORTUNATELY, TODAY'S CARD FLIP TIME IS OVER.
HUH ?!
COME NOW. DON'T BE TOO DISAP-POINTED!!
Tsk tsk.

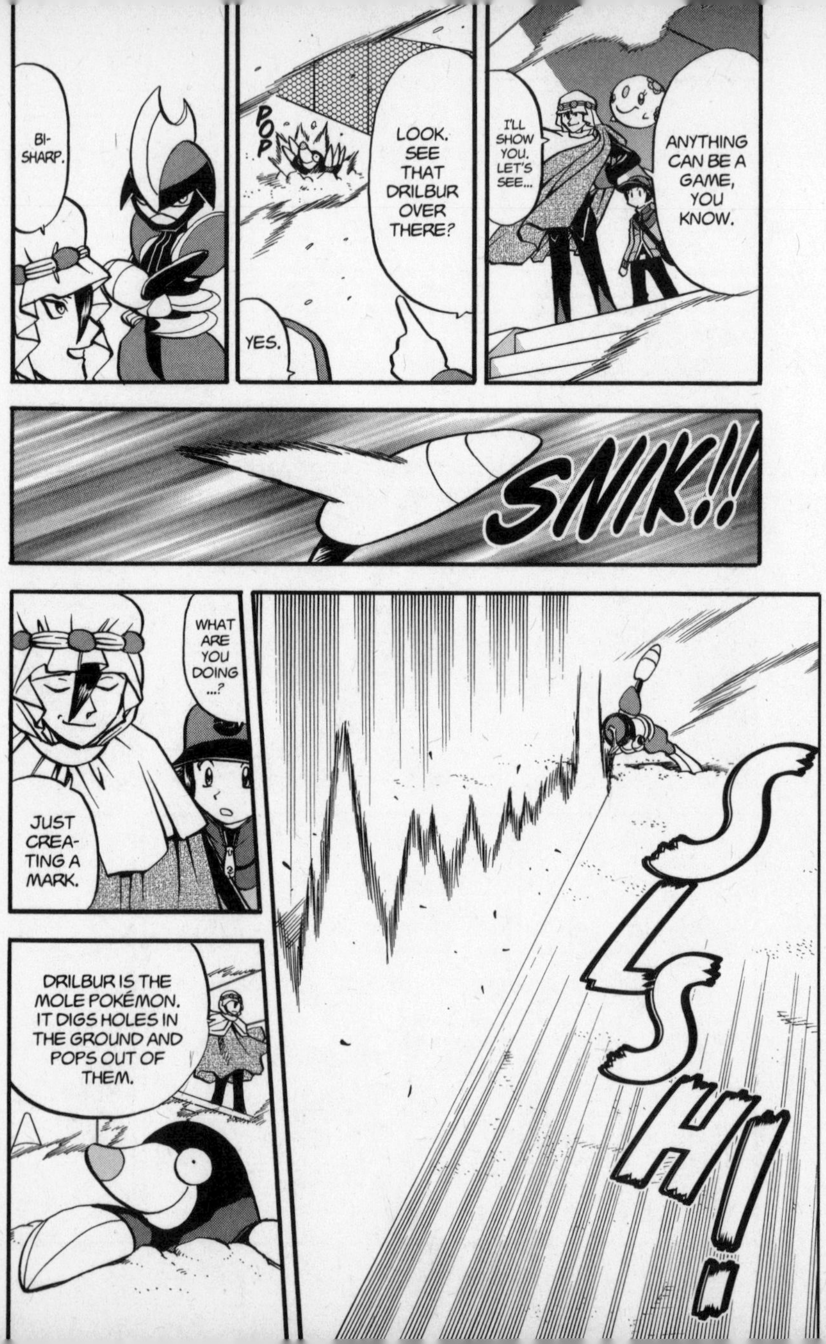
ANYTHING CAN BE A GAME, YOU KNOW.
I'LL SHOW YOU. LET'S SEE...
POP
POP
LOOK. SEE THAT DRILBUR OVER THERE?
YES.
BI-SHARP.
SNIK!!
SLASH!
WHAT ARE YOU DOING...?
JUST CREATING A MARK.
DRILBUR IS THE MOLE POKÉMON. IT DIGS HOLES IN THE GROUND AND POPS OUT OF THEM.

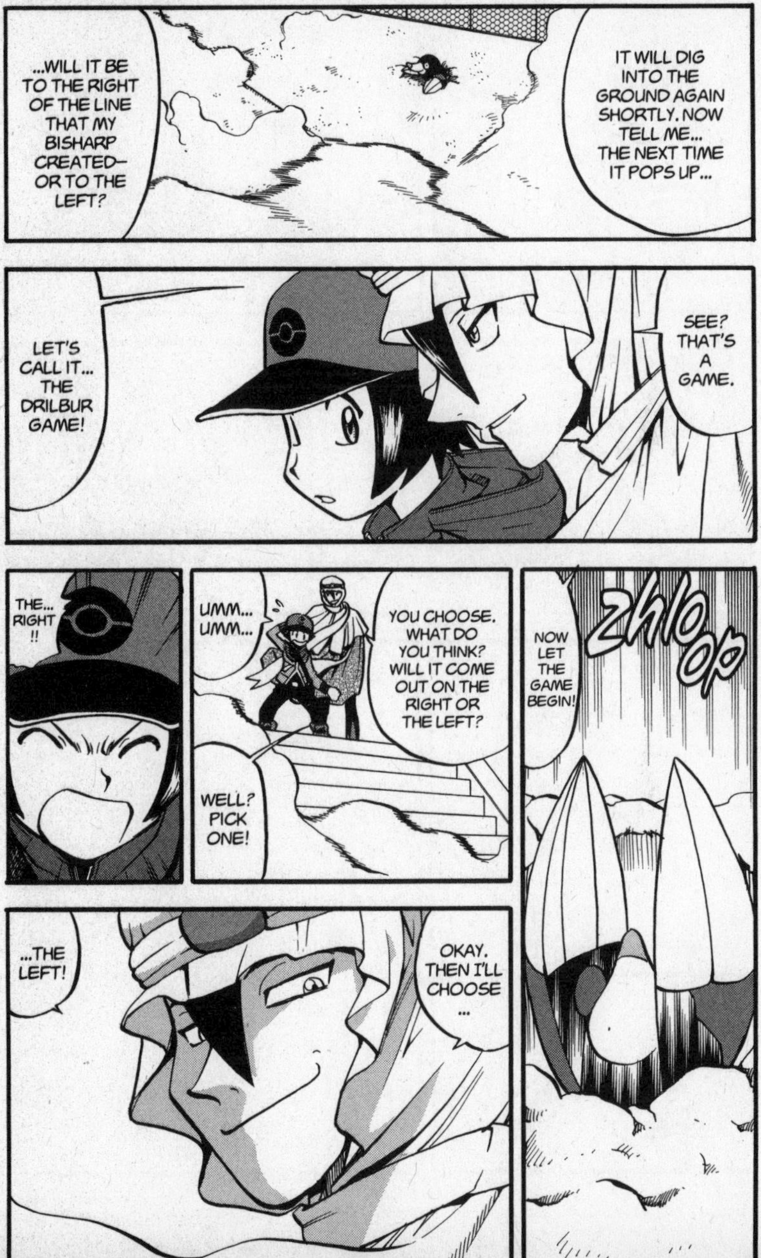
IT WILL DIG INTO THE GROUND AGAIN SHORTLY. NOW TELL ME... THE NEXT TIME IT POPS UP...
...WILL IT BE TO THE RIGHT OF THE LINE THAT MY BISHARP CREATED– OR TO THE LEFT?
SEE? THAT'S A GAME.
LET'S CALL IT... THE DRILBUR GAME!
ZHLOOP
NOW LET THE GAME BEGIN!
YOU CHOOSE. WHAT DO YOU THINK? WILL IT COME OUT ON THE RIGHT OR THE LEFT?
UMM... UMM...
WELL? PICK ONE!
THE... RIGHT !!
OKAY. THEN I'LL CHOOSE ...
...THE LEFT!

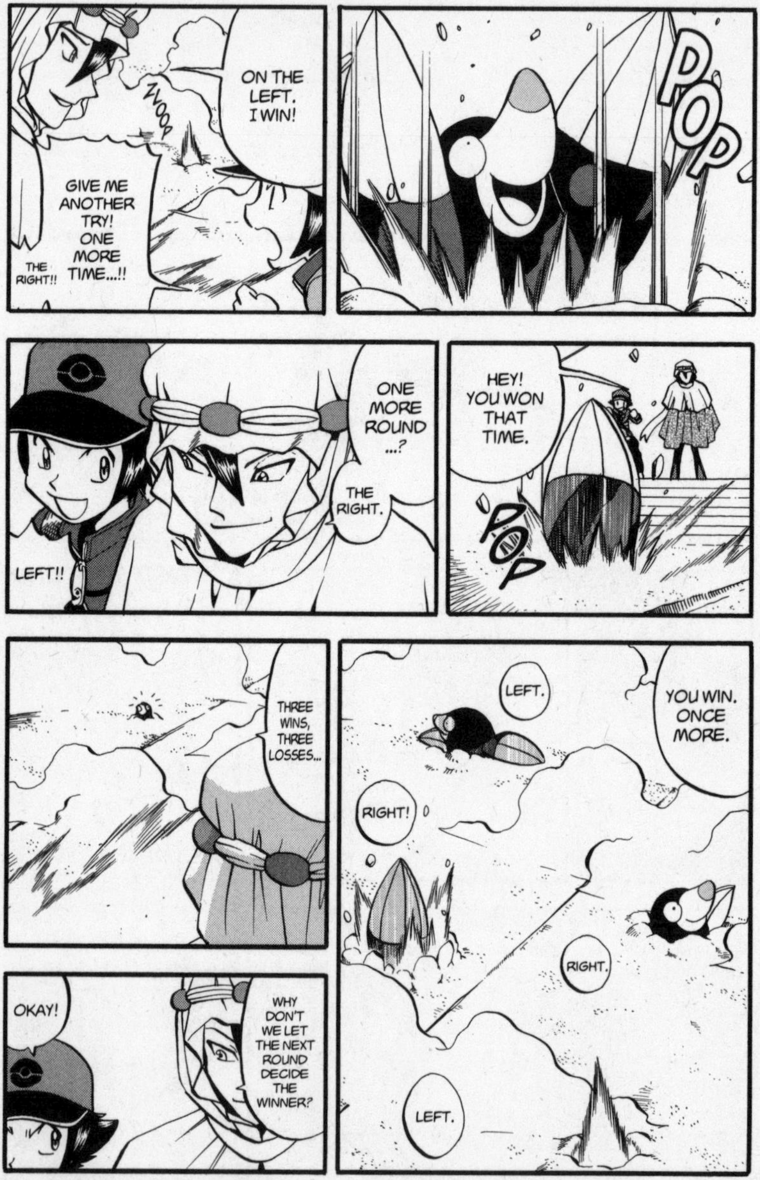
POP
POP
ON THE LEFT. I WIN!
ZVOOP
GIVE ME ANOTHER TRY! ONE MORE TIME...!!
THE RIGHT!!
HEY! YOU WON THAT TIME.
POP
POP
ONE MORE ROUND ...?
THE RIGHT.
LEFT!!
YOU WIN. ONCE MORE.
LEFT.
RIGHT!
RIGHT.
LEFT.
THREE WINS, THREE LOSSES...
WHY DON'T WE LET THE NEXT ROUND DECIDE THE WINNER?
OKAY!

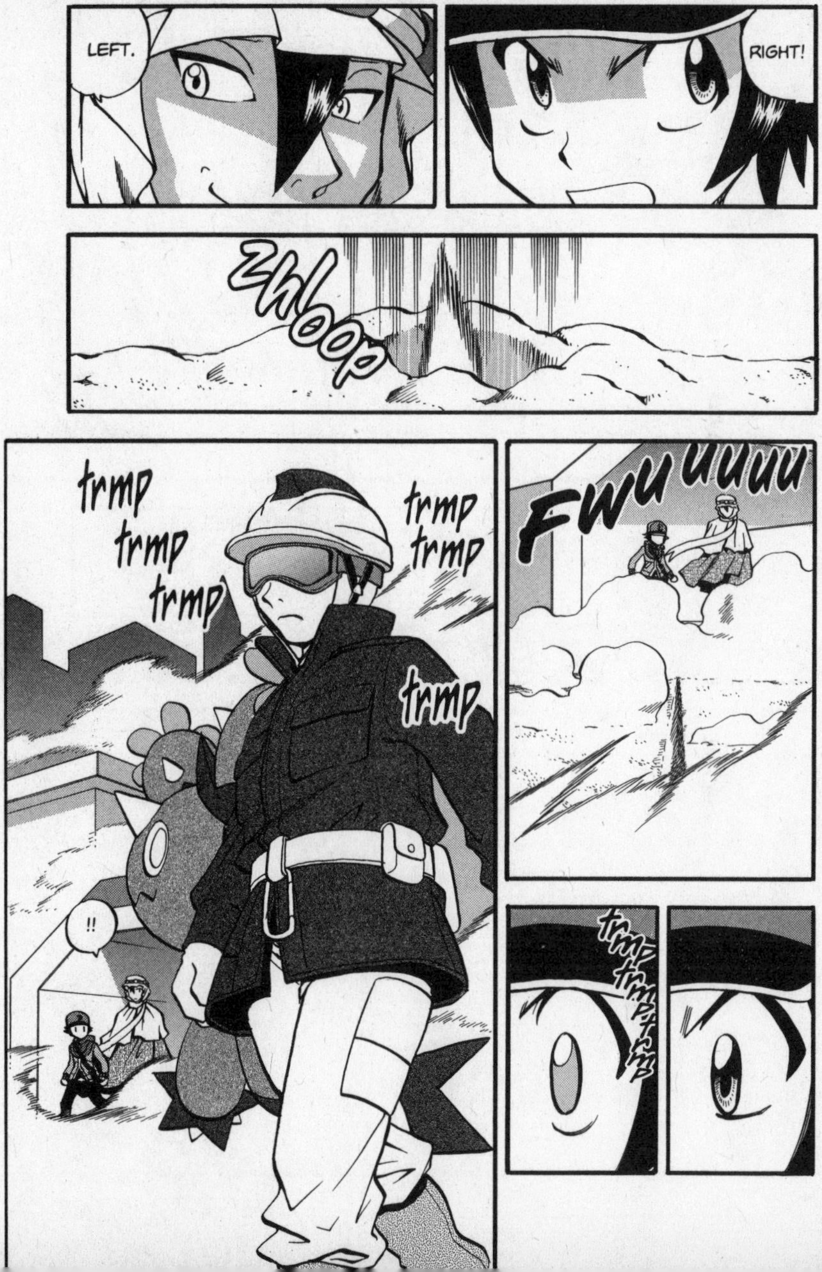
RIGHT!
LEFT.
zhloop
trmp
trmp
trmp
trmp
trmp
trmp
!!
Fwuuuuuu
trmp trmp trmp

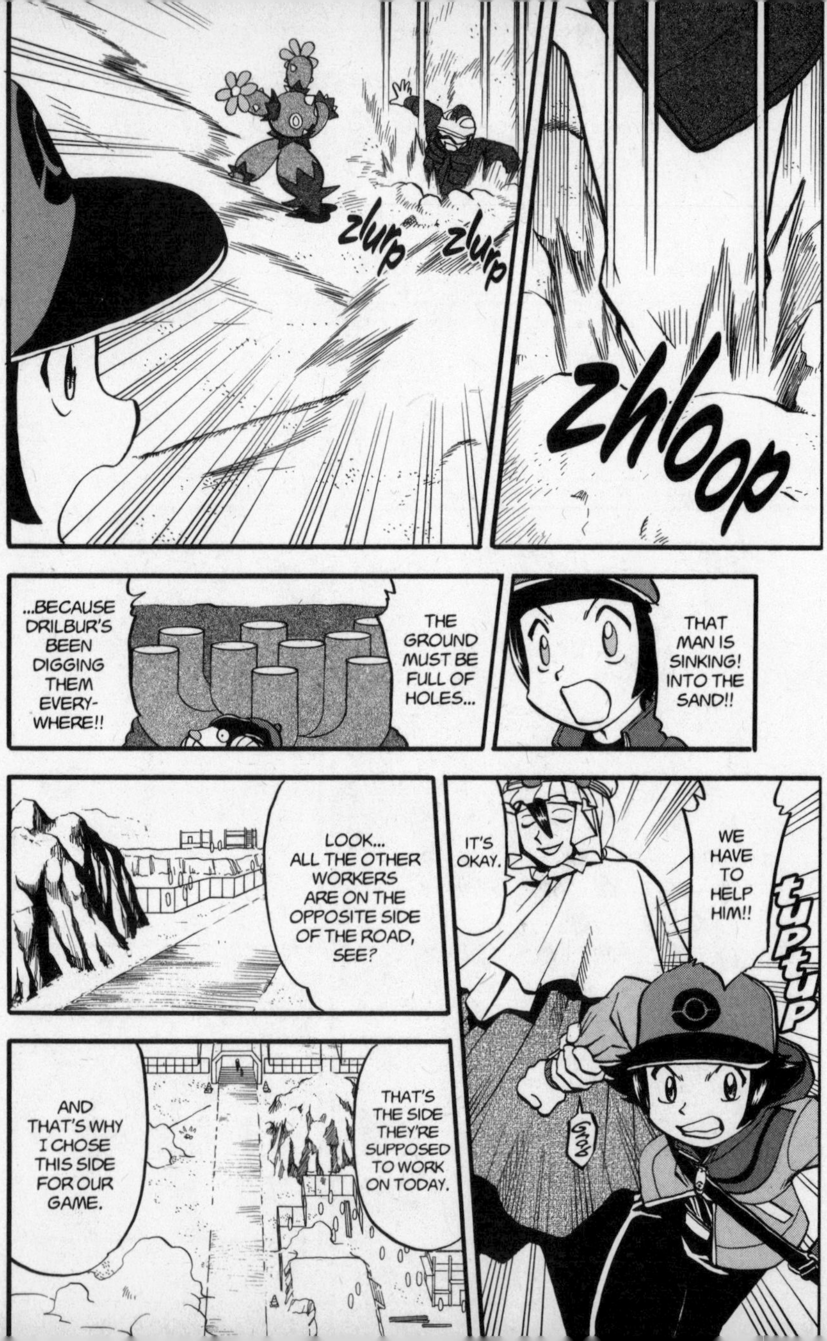
zhloop
zlurp
zlurp
THAT MAN IS SINKING! INTO THE SAND!!
THE GROUND MUST BE FULL OF HOLES...
...BECAUSE DRILBUR'S BEEN DIGGING THEM EVERY-WHERE!!
WE HAVE TO HELP HIM!!
tup tup
IT'S OKAY.
GRAB
LOOK... ALL THE OTHER WORKERS ARE ON THE OPPOSITE SIDE OF THE ROAD, SEE?
THAT'S THE SIDE THEY'RE SUPPOSED TO WORK ON TODAY.
AND THAT'S WHY I CHOSE THIS SIDE FOR OUR GAME.

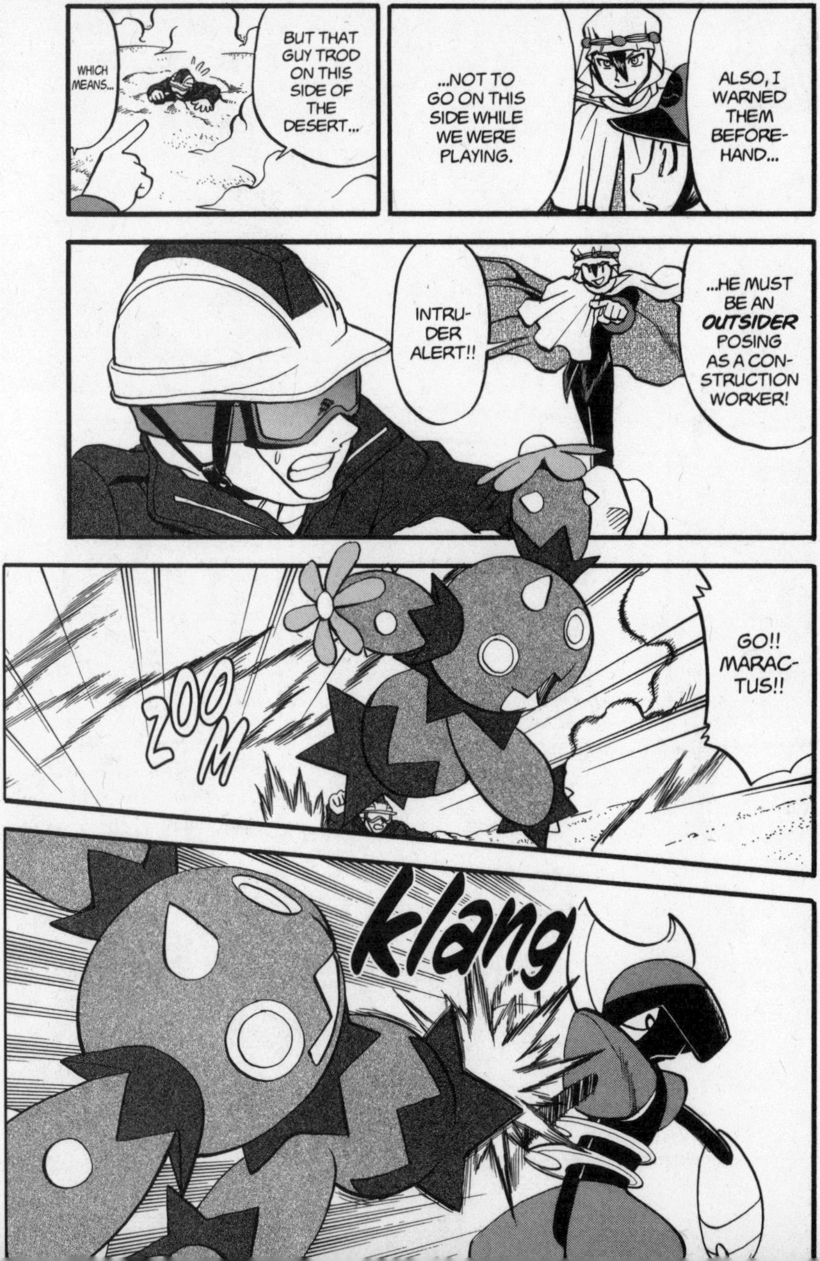
WHICH MEANS...
BUT THAT GUY TROD ON THIS SIDE OF THE DESERT...
...NOT TO GO ON THIS SIDE WHILE WE WERE PLAYING.
ALSO, I WARNED THEM BEFORE-HAND...
INTRU-DER ALERT!!
...HE MUST BE AN OUTSIDER POSING AS A CON-STRUCTION WORKER!
ZOOM
GO!! MARAC-TUS!!
klang

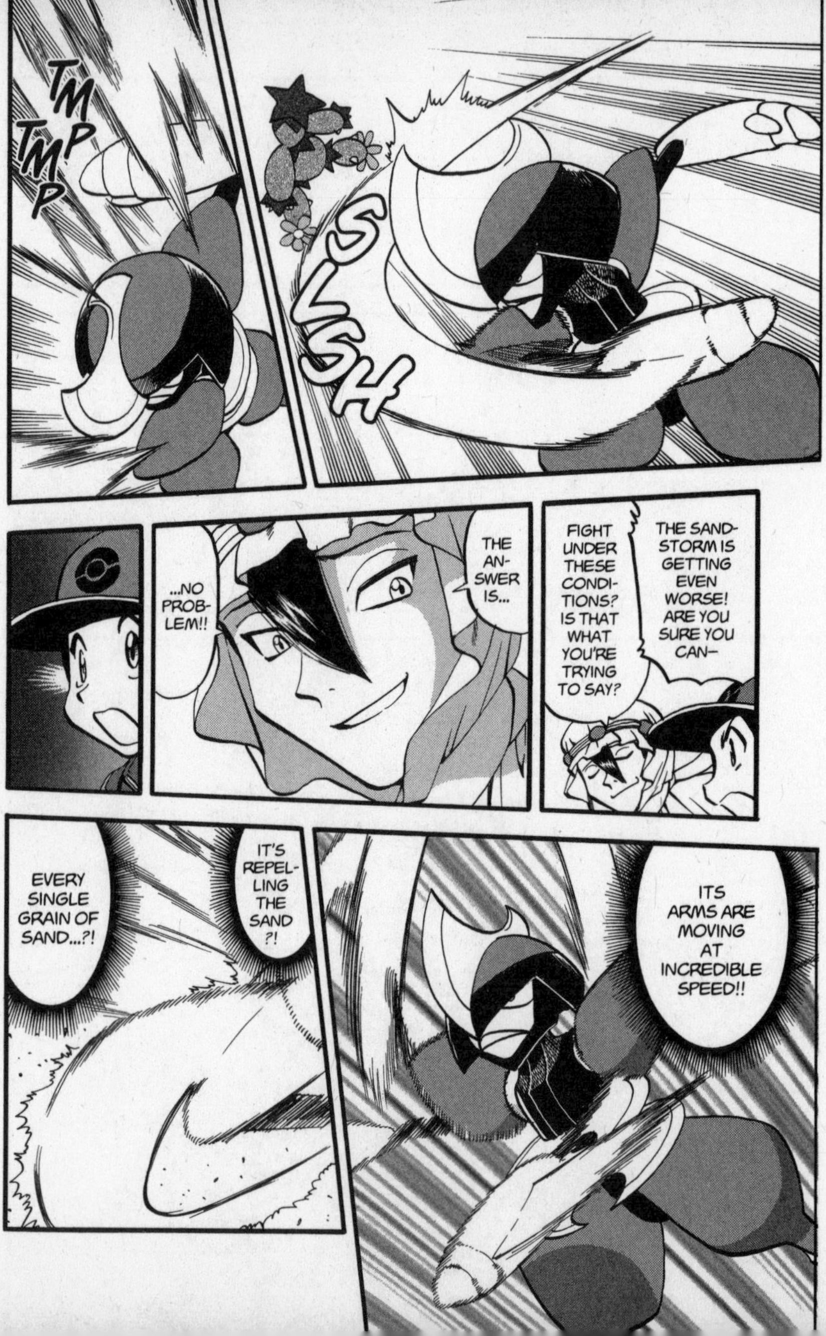
TMP TMP
SLSH
THE SAND-STORM IS GETTING EVEN WORSE! ARE YOU SURE YOU CAN—
FIGHT UNDER THESE CONDI-TIONS? IS THAT WHAT YOU'RE TRYING TO SAY?
THE AN-SWER IS...
...NO PROB-LEM!!
ITS ARMS ARE MOVING AT INCREDIBLE SPEED!!
IT'S REPEL-LING THE SAND ?!
EVERY SINGLE GRAIN OF SAND...?!

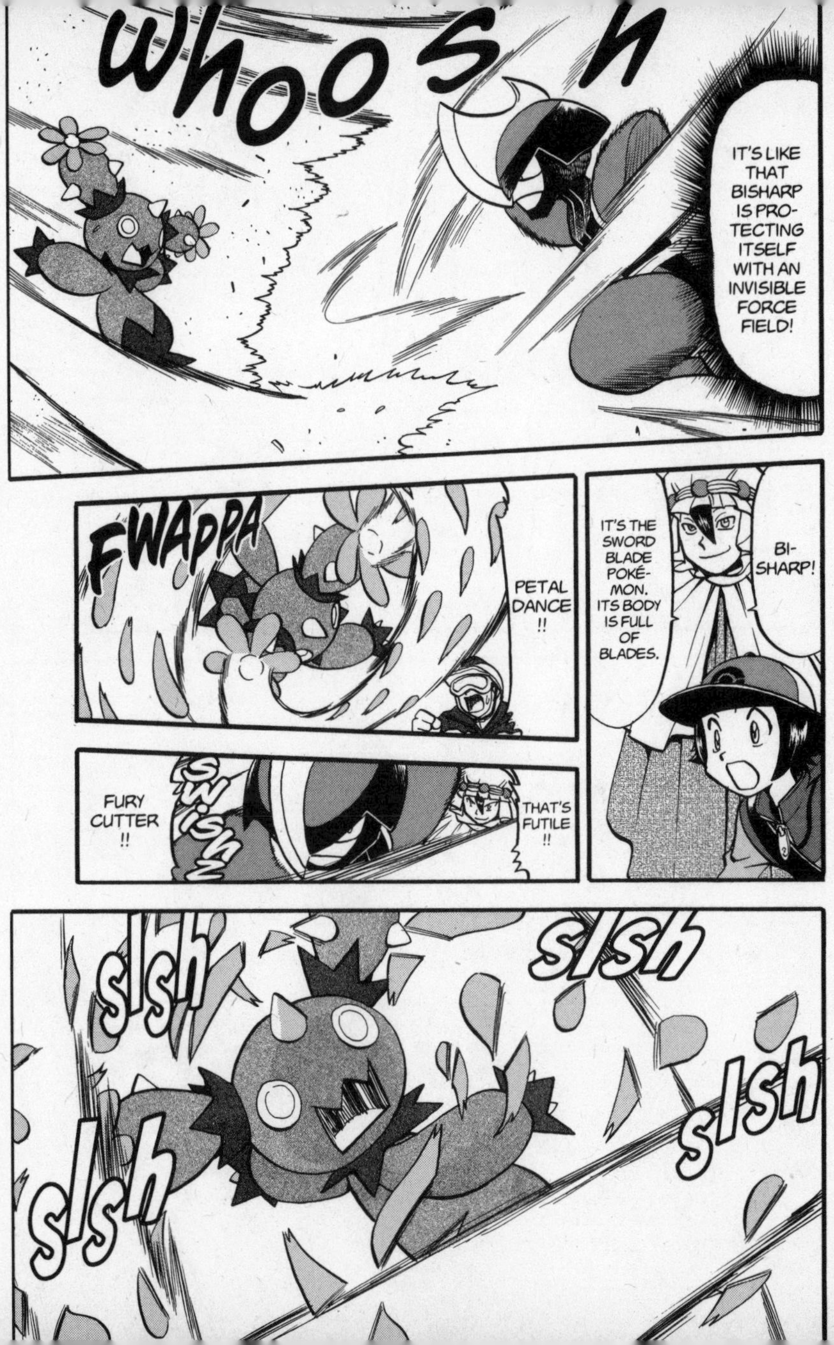
WHOOSH
IT'S LIKE THAT BISHARP IS PROTECTING ITSELF WITH AN INVISIBLE FORCE FIELD!
FWAPPA
PETAL DANCE!!
BI-SHARP!
IT'S THE SWORD BLADE POKÉMON. ITS BODY IS FULL OF BLADES.
FURY CUTTER!!
SWISH
THAT'S FUTILE!!
slsh
slsh
slsh
slsh

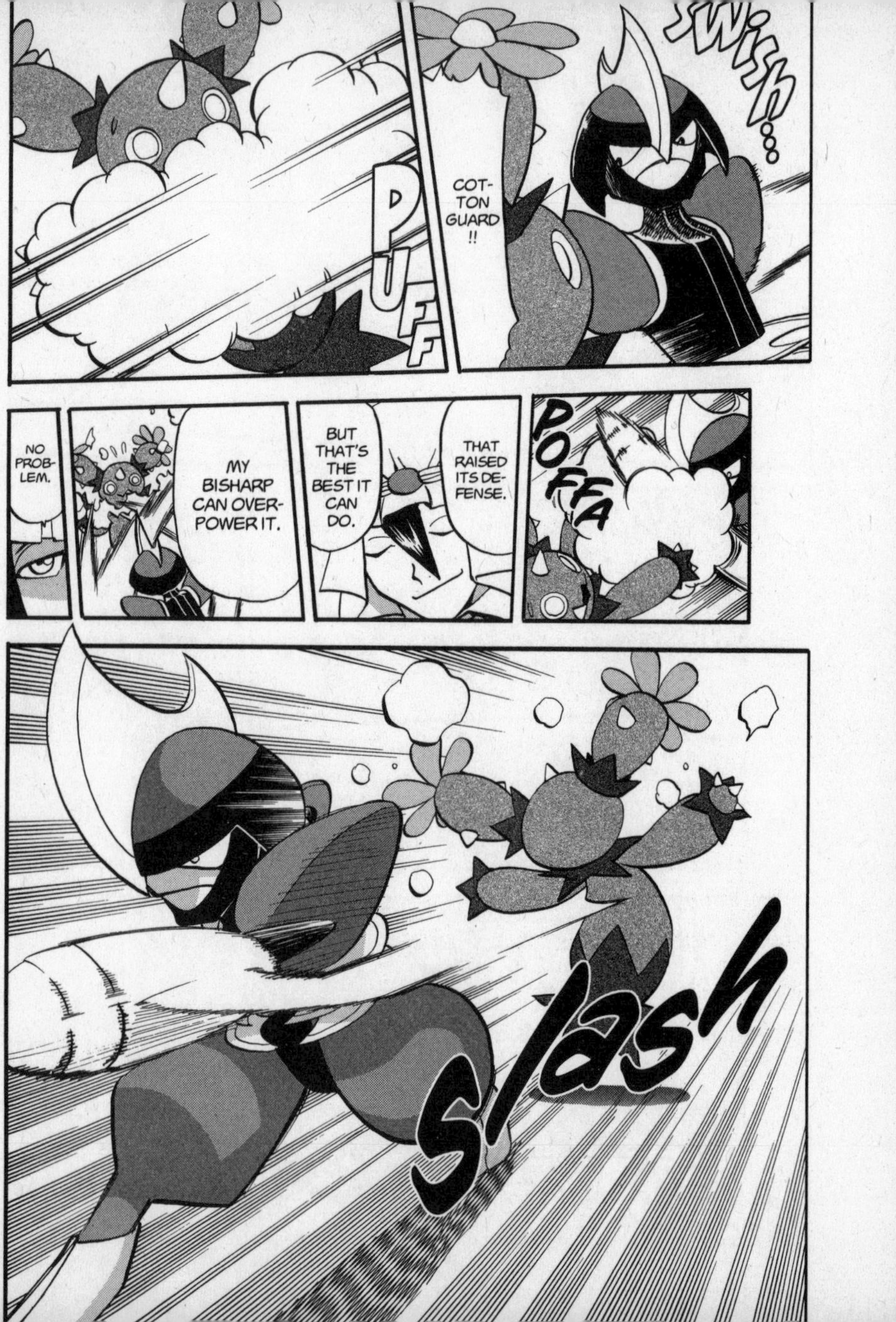
PUFF
COTTON GUARD!!
SWISH...
NO PROBLEM.
MY BISHARP CAN OVERPOWER IT.
BUT THAT'S THE BEST IT CAN DO.
THAT RAISED ITS DEFENSE.
POFFA
Slash

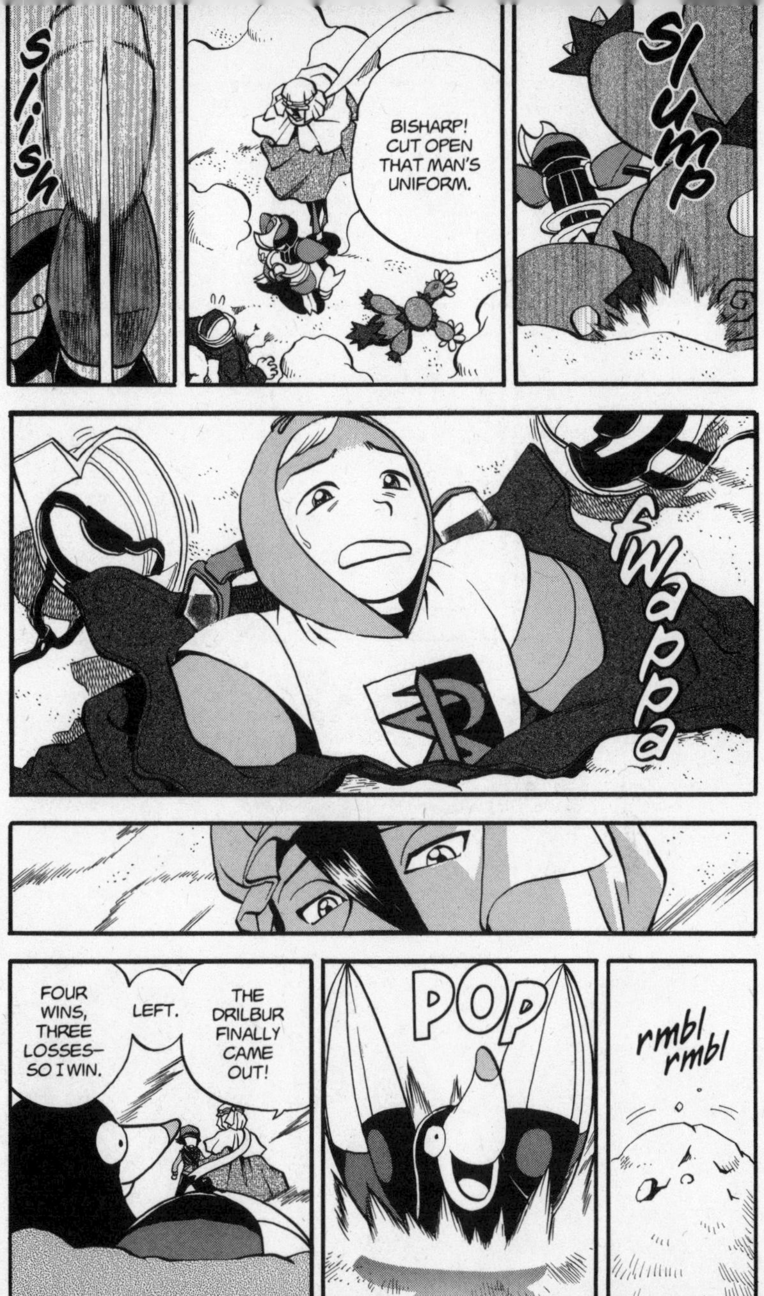
Slish
BISHARP! CUT OPEN THAT MAN'S UNIFORM.
Slump
fwappa
FOUR WINS, THREE LOSSES— SO I WIN.
LEFT.
THE DRILBUR FINALLY CAME OUT!
POP
rmbl rmbl

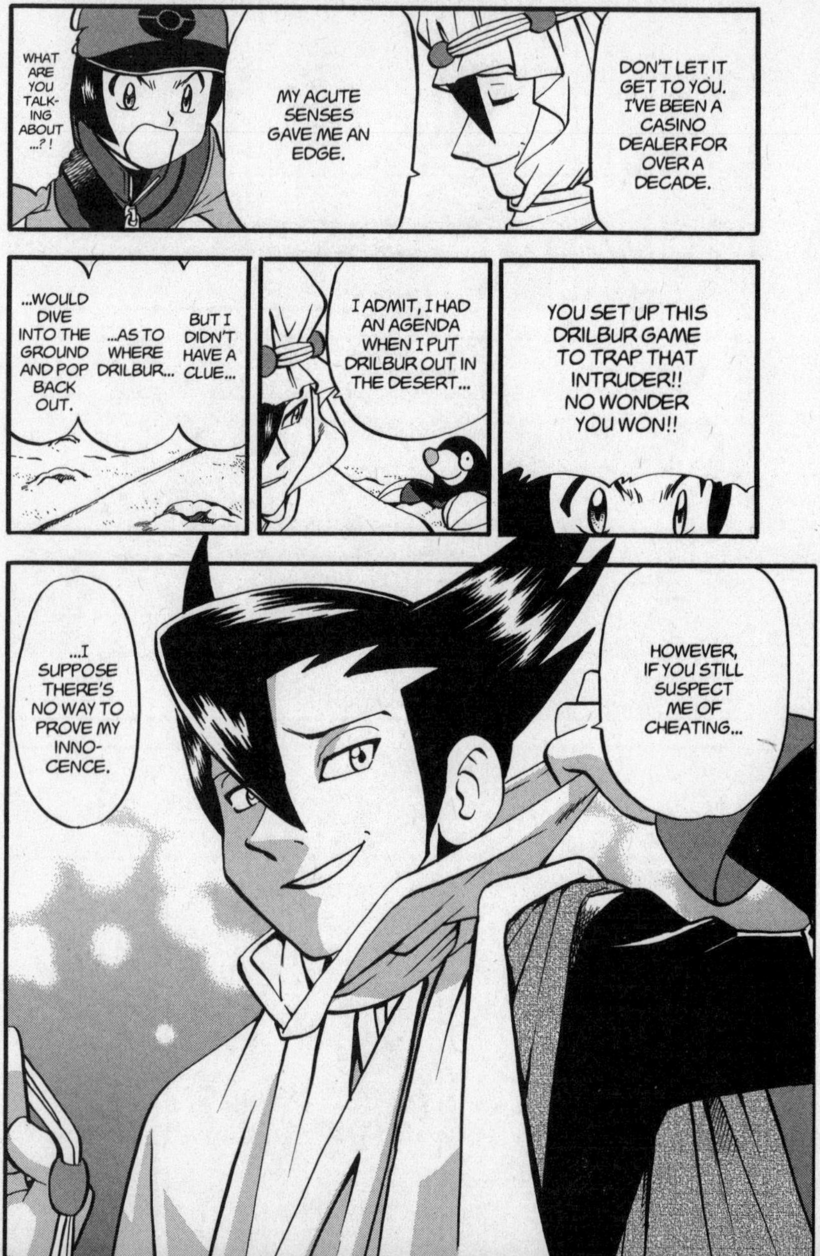
DON'T LET IT GET TO YOU. I'VE BEEN A CASINO DEALER FOR OVER A DECADE.
MY ACUTE SENSES GAVE ME AN EDGE.
WHAT ARE YOU TALKING ABOUT...?!
YOU SET UP THIS DRILBUR GAME TO TRAP THAT INTRUDER!! NO WONDER YOU WON!!
I ADMIT, I HAD AN AGENDA WHEN I PUT DRILBUR OUT IN THE DESERT...
BUT I DIDN'T HAVE A CLUE...
...AS TO WHERE DRILBUR...
...WOULD DIVE INTO THE GROUND AND POP BACK OUT.
HOWEVER, IF YOU STILL SUSPECT ME OF CHEATING...
...I SUPPOSE THERE'S NO WAY TO PROVE MY INNOCENCE.

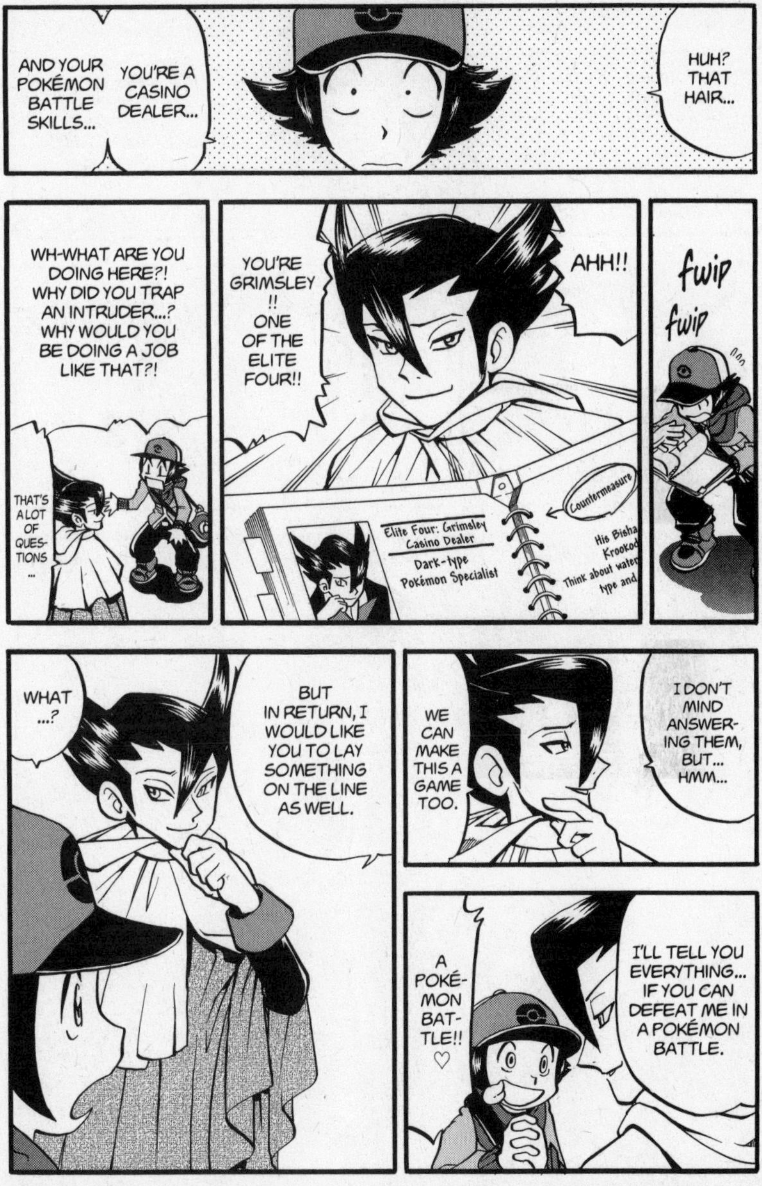

HUH? THAT HAIR...
YOU'RE A CASINO DEALER...
AND YOUR POKÉMON BATTLE SKILLS...
fwip
fwip
AHH!!
YOU'RE GRIMSLEY!! ONE OF THE ELITE FOUR!!
Countermeasure
Elite Four: Grimsley
Casino Dealer
Dark-type
Pokémon Specialist
His Bisha
Krookod
Think about water
type and
WH-WHAT ARE YOU DOING HERE?! WHY DID YOU TRAP AN INTRUDER...? WHY WOULD YOU BE DOING A JOB LIKE THAT?!
THAT'S A LOT OF QUES-TIONS...
I DON'T MIND ANSWER-ING THEM, BUT... HMM...
WE CAN MAKE THIS A GAME TOO.
BUT IN RETURN, I WOULD LIKE YOU TO LAY SOMETHING ON THE LINE AS WELL.
WHAT ...?
I'LL TELL YOU EVERYTHING... IF YOU CAN DEFEAT ME IN A POKÉMON BATTLE.
A POKÉ-MON BAT-TLE!! ♡

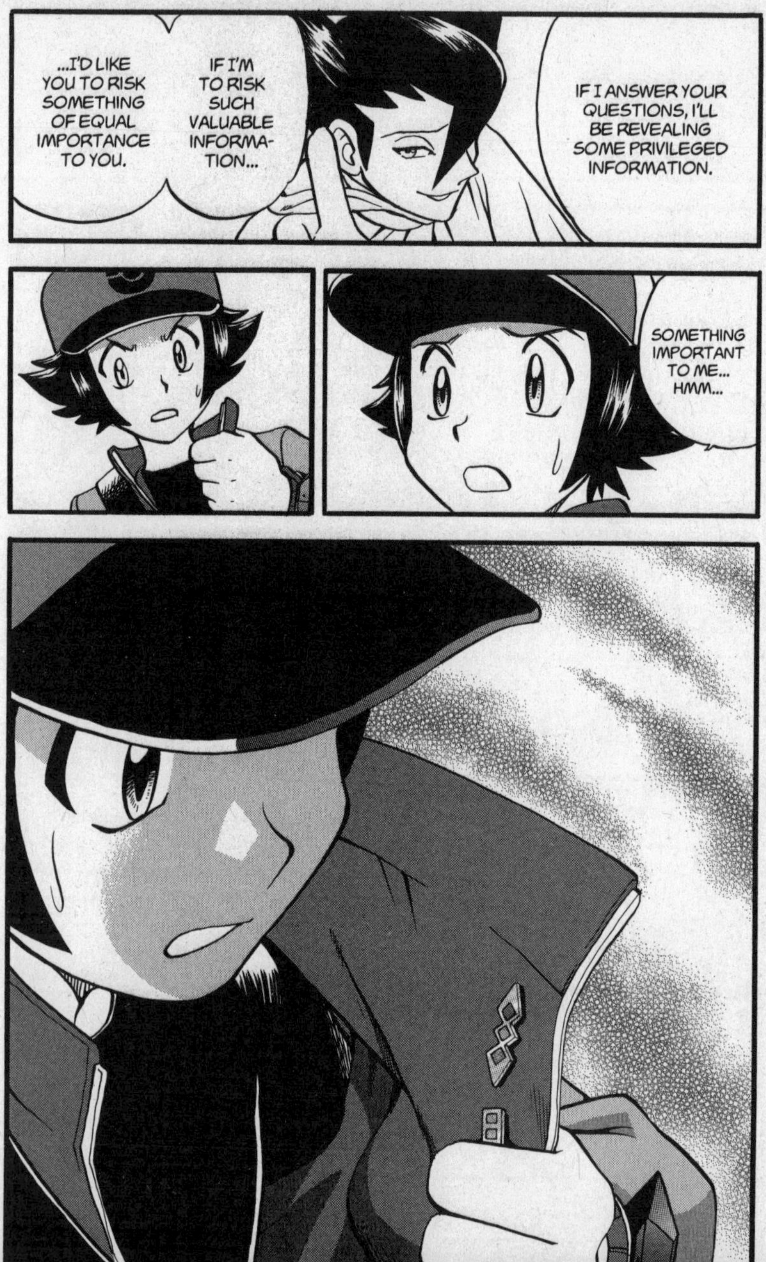
IF I ANSWER YOUR QUESTIONS, I'LL BE REVEALING SOME PRIVILEGED INFORMATION.
IF I'M TO RISK SUCH VALUABLE INFORMA-TION...
...I'D LIKE YOU TO RISK SOMETHING OF EQUAL IMPORTANCE TO YOU.
SOMETHING IMPORTANT TO ME... HMM...

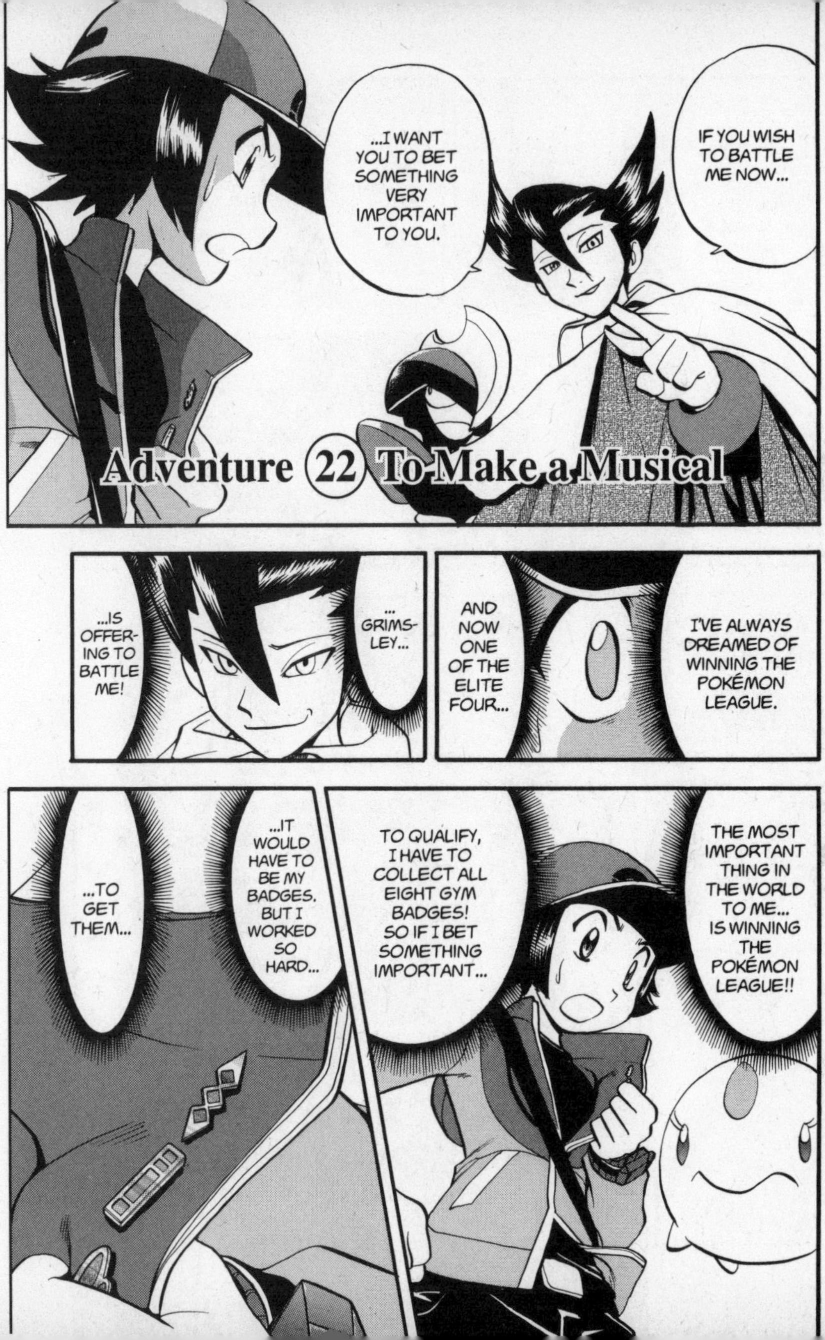
IF YOU WISH TO BATTLE ME NOW...
...I WANT YOU TO BET SOMETHING VERY IMPORTANT TO YOU.
Adventure 22 To Make a Musical
I'VE ALWAYS DREAMED OF WINNING THE POKÉMON LEAGUE.
AND NOW ONE OF THE ELITE FOUR...
... GRIMS-LEY...
...IS OFFER-ING TO BATTLE ME!
THE MOST IMPORTANT THING IN THE WORLD TO ME... IS WINNING THE POKÉMON LEAGUE!!
TO QUALIFY, I HAVE TO COLLECT ALL EIGHT GYM BADGES! SO IF I BET SOMETHING IMPORTANT...
...IT WOULD HAVE TO BE MY BADGES. BUT I WORKED SO HARD...
...TO GET THEM...

 ...I'D LOSE MY CHANCE OF ENTER- ING THE POKÉMON LEAGUE!!

AND THEN...

 ...IF I LOST, I'D HAVE TO GIVE THEM UP...

BETTING THEM WOULD MEAN...

 WHAT TO DO?! WHAT TO DO?!

(Huf.)

(Huf.)

WHAT SHOULD I DO ...?!

 Boom!

 H- HEY...

fwump

 to ...e a battle but to put my badges ... the line ...won't be my bad... ...the able ....m ...lose ...t c... then but if I lo... my badges... I won't ... but I w... ...ba... ...ut I ...ed to ...y badges... the

URGH!

ARGH!

 EH? ARE YOU ALL RIGHT, YOUNG MAN?

Huf.

Huf.

Adventure 22 To Make a Musical

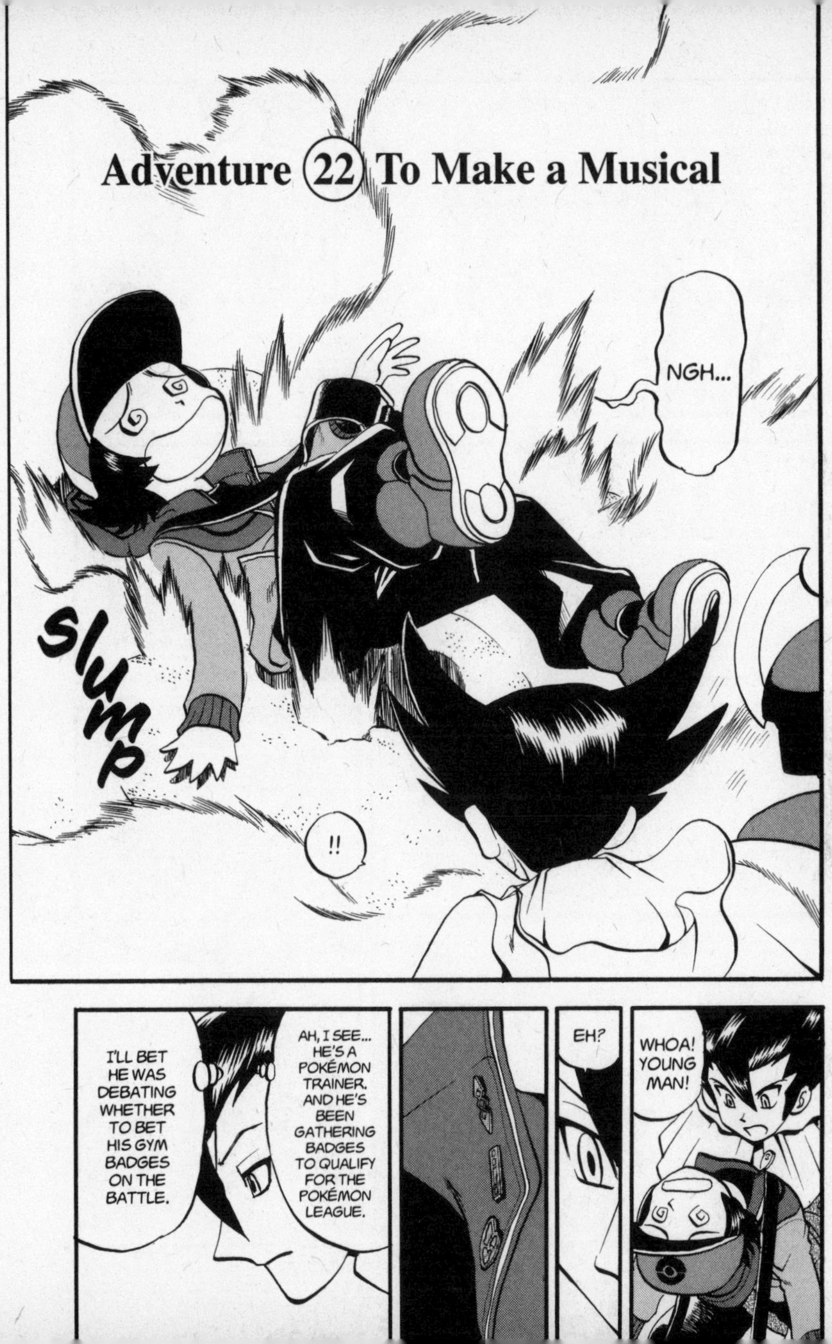
NGH...
slump
!!
WHOA! YOUNG MAN!
EH?
AH, I SEE... HE'S A POKÉMON TRAINER. AND HE'S BEEN GATHERING BADGES TO QUALIFY FOR THE POKÉMON LEAGUE.
I'LL BET HE WAS DEBATING WHETHER TO BET HIS GYM BADGES ON THE BATTLE.

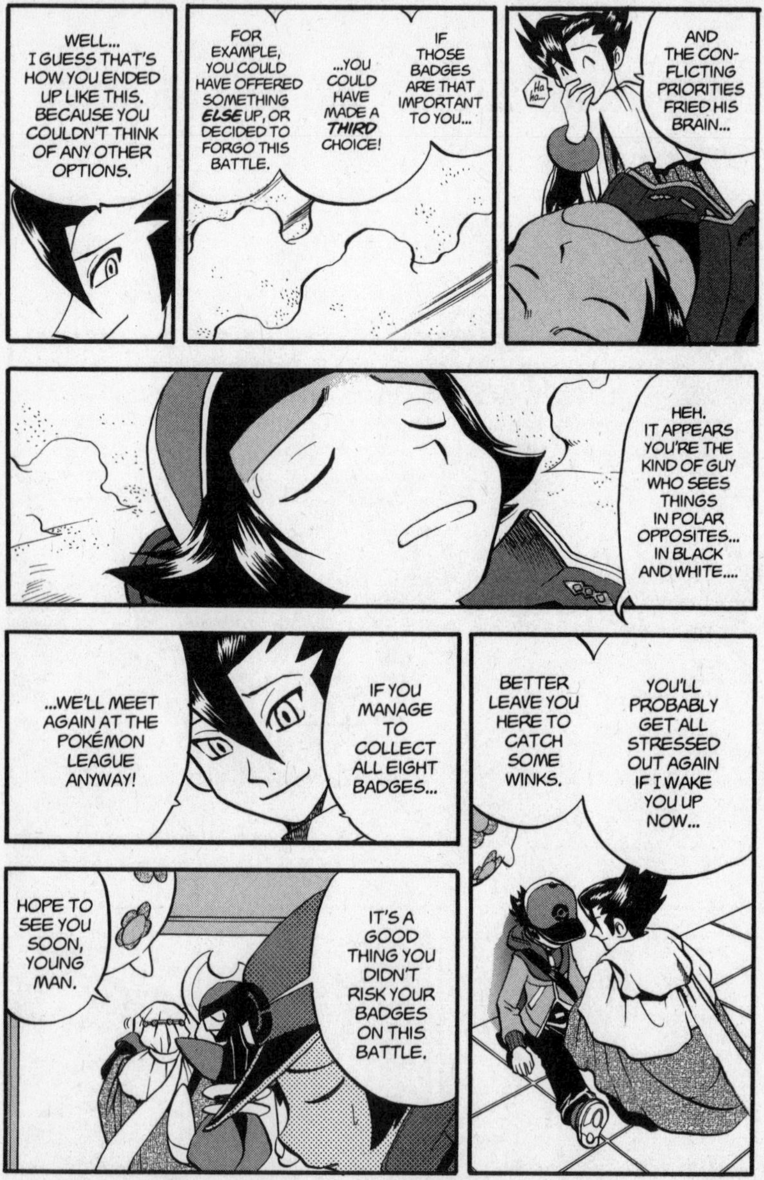

AND THE CON-FLICTING PRIORITIES FRIED HIS BRAIN...
Ha ha...
IF THOSE BADGES ARE THAT IMPORTANT TO YOU...
...YOU COULD HAVE MADE A THIRD CHOICE!
FOR EXAMPLE, YOU COULD HAVE OFFERED SOMETHING ELSE UP, OR DECIDED TO FORGO THIS BATTLE.
WELL... I GUESS THAT'S HOW YOU ENDED UP LIKE THIS. BECAUSE YOU COULDN'T THINK OF ANY OTHER OPTIONS.
HEH. IT APPEARS YOU'RE THE KIND OF GUY WHO SEES THINGS IN POLAR OPPOSITES... IN BLACK AND WHITE....
YOU'LL PROBABLY GET ALL STRESSED OUT AGAIN IF I WAKE YOU UP NOW...
BETTER LEAVE YOU HERE TO CATCH SOME WINKS.
IF YOU MANAGE TO COLLECT ALL EIGHT BADGES...
...WE'LL MEET AGAIN AT THE POKÉMON LEAGUE ANYWAY!
IT'S A GOOD THING YOU DIDN'T RISK YOUR BADGES ON THIS BATTLE.
HOPE TO SEE YOU SOON, YOUNG MAN.

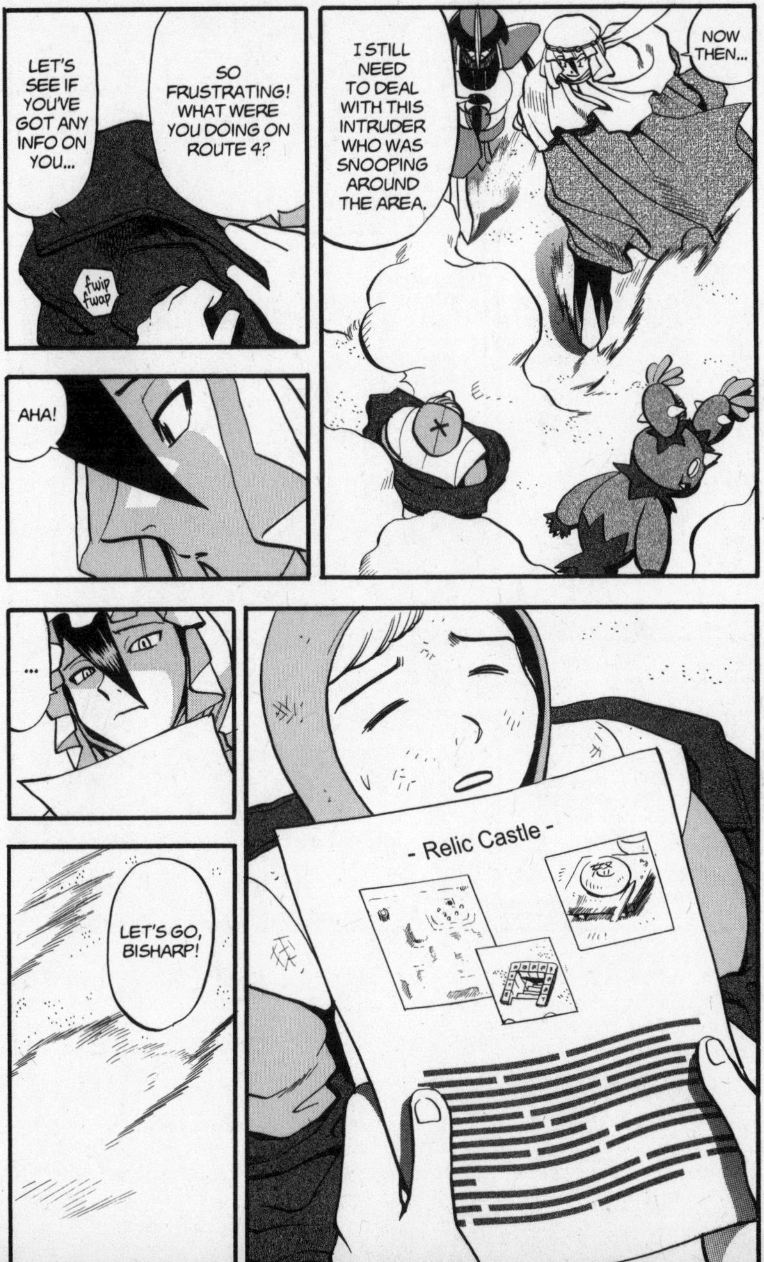
NOW THEN...
I STILL NEED TO DEAL WITH THIS INTRUDER WHO WAS SNOOPING AROUND THE AREA.
SO FRUSTRATING! WHAT WERE YOU DOING ON ROUTE 4?
LET'S SEE IF YOU'VE GOT ANY INFO ON YOU...
fwip fwap
AHA!
...
- Relic Castle -
LET'S GO, BISHARP!

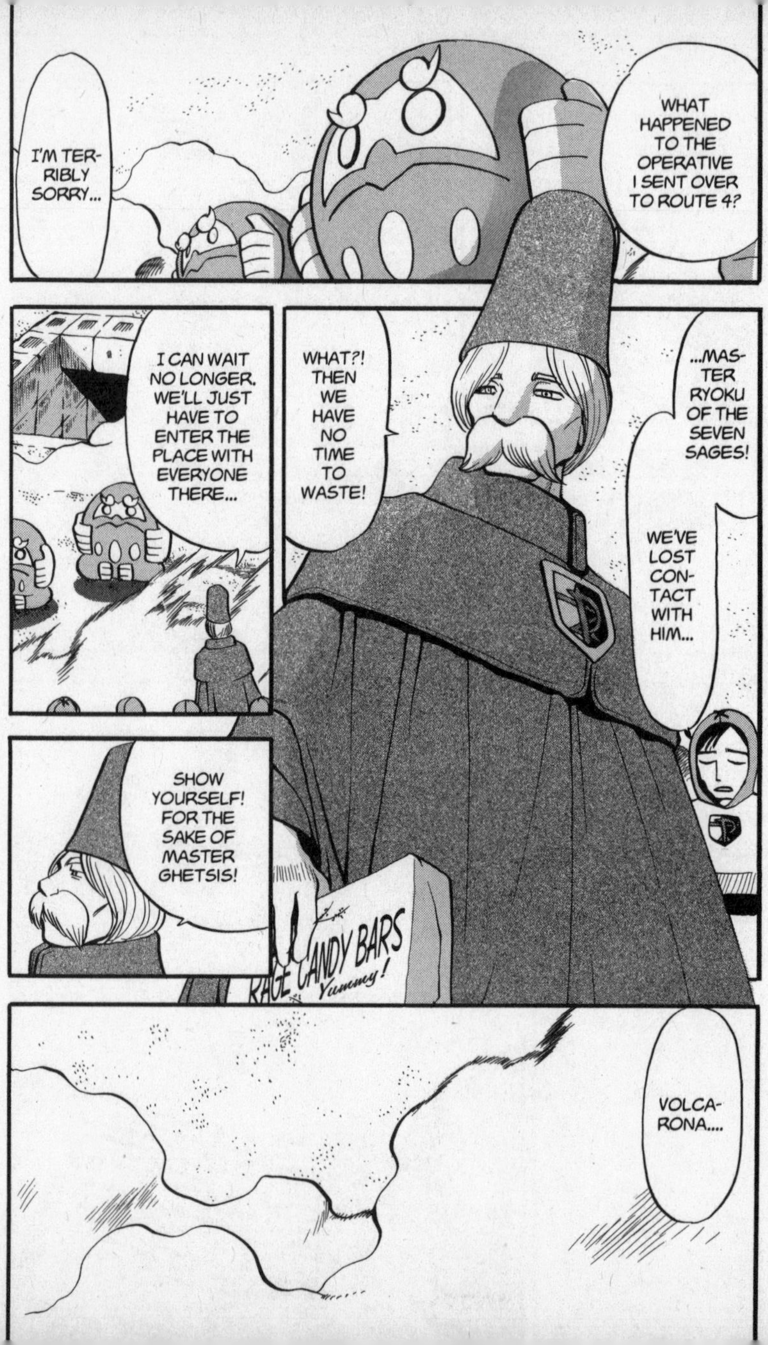
I'M TERRIBLY SORRY...
WHAT HAPPENED TO THE OPERATIVE I SENT OVER TO ROUTE 4?
...MASTER RYOKU OF THE SEVEN SAGES!
WE'VE LOST CONTACT WITH HIM...
WHAT?! THEN WE HAVE NO TIME TO WASTE!
I CAN WAIT NO LONGER. WE'LL JUST HAVE TO ENTER THE PLACE WITH EVERYONE THERE...
SHOW YOURSELF! FOR THE SAKE OF MASTER GHETSIS!
RAGE CANDY BARS
Yummy!
VOLCARONA....

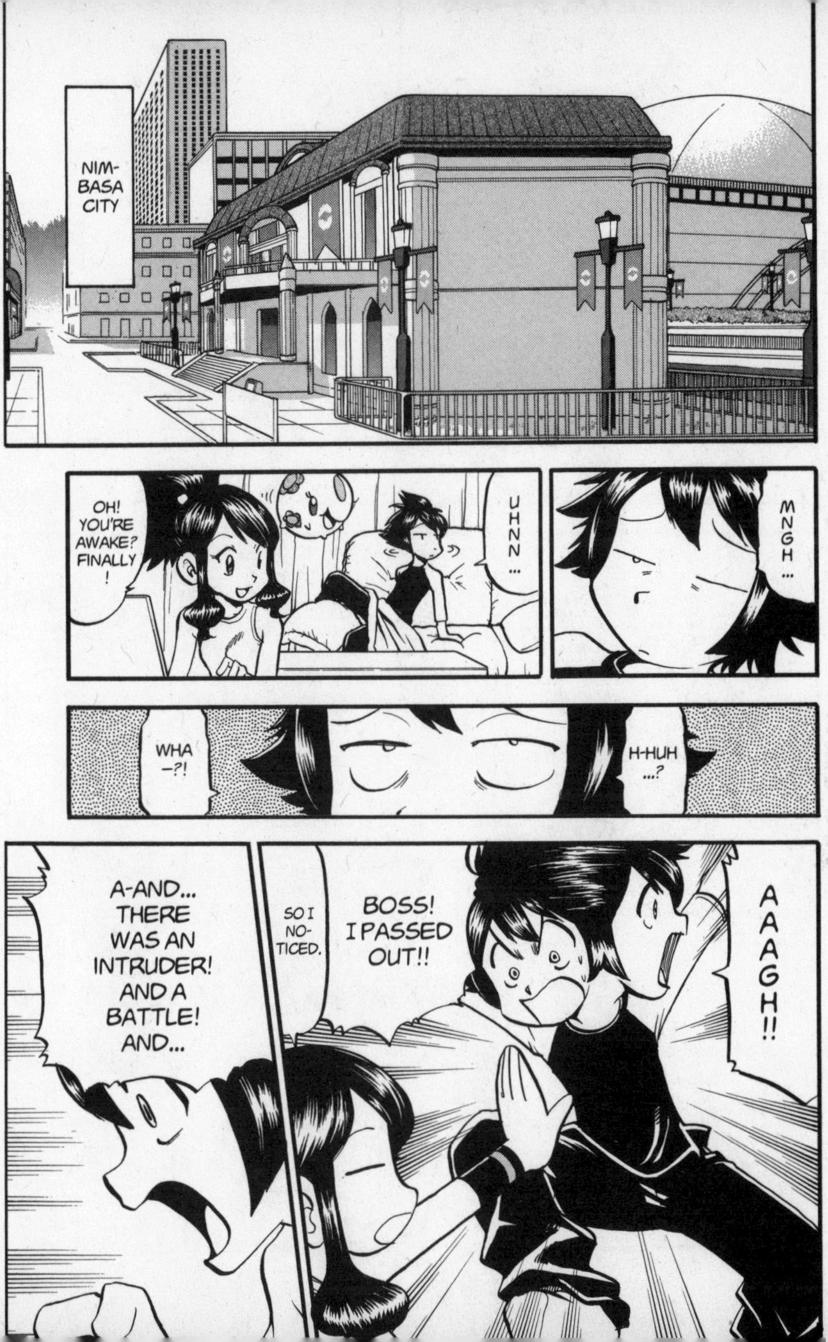
NIMBASA CITY
MNGH...
UHNN...
OH! YOU'RE AWAKE? FINALLY!
H-HUH...?
WHA-?!
AAAGH!!
BOSS! I PASSED OUT!!
SO I NOTICED.
A-AND... THERE WAS AN INTRUDER! AND A BATTLE! AND...

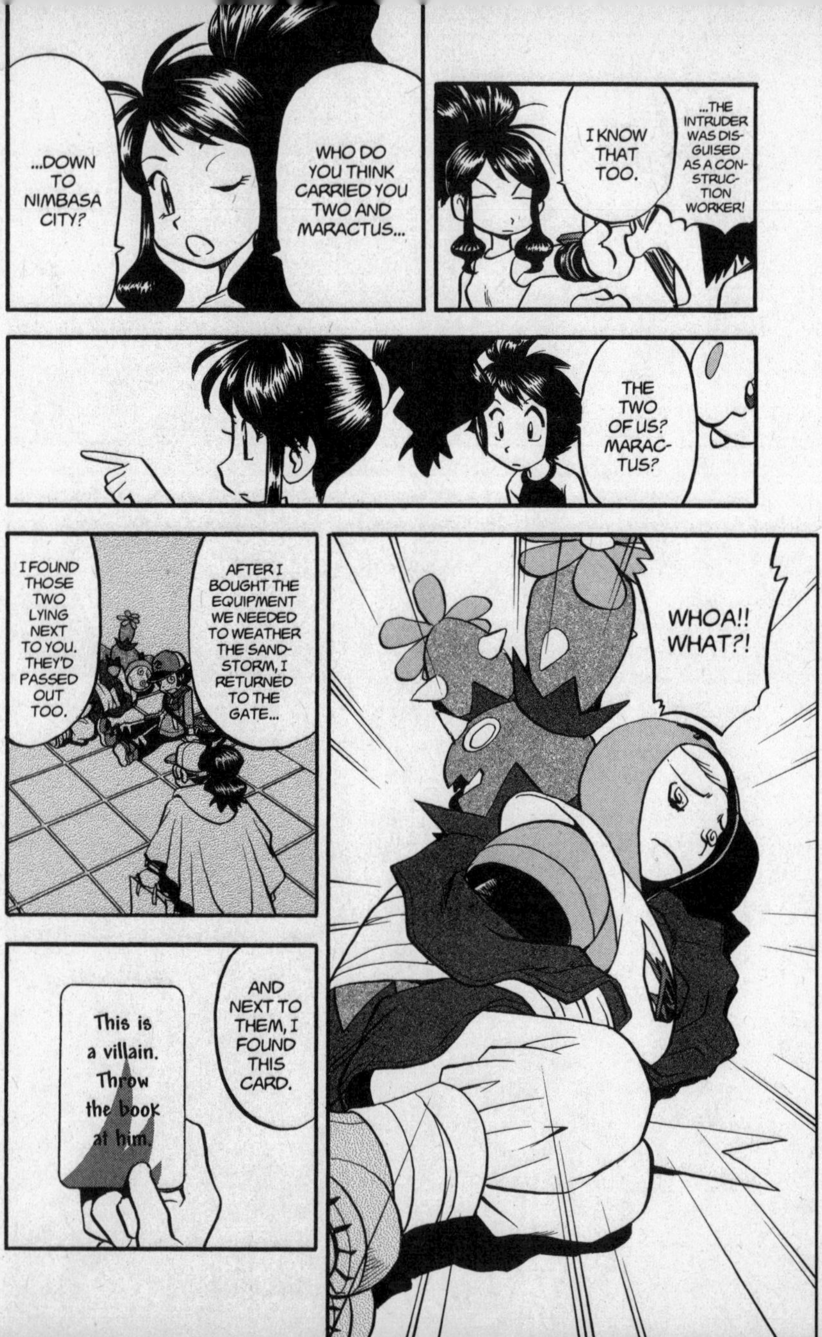
...DOWN TO NIMBASA CITY?
WHO DO YOU THINK CARRIED YOU TWO AND MARACTUS...
I KNOW THAT TOO.
...THE INTRUDER WAS DISGUISED AS A CONSTRUCTION WORKER!
THE TWO OF US? MARACTUS?
AFTER I BOUGHT THE EQUIPMENT WE NEEDED TO WEATHER THE SANDSTORM, I RETURNED TO THE GATE...
I FOUND THOSE TWO LYING NEXT TO YOU. THEY'D PASSED OUT TOO.
WHOA!! WHAT?!
AND NEXT TO THEM, I FOUND THIS CARD.
This is a villain. Throw the book at him.

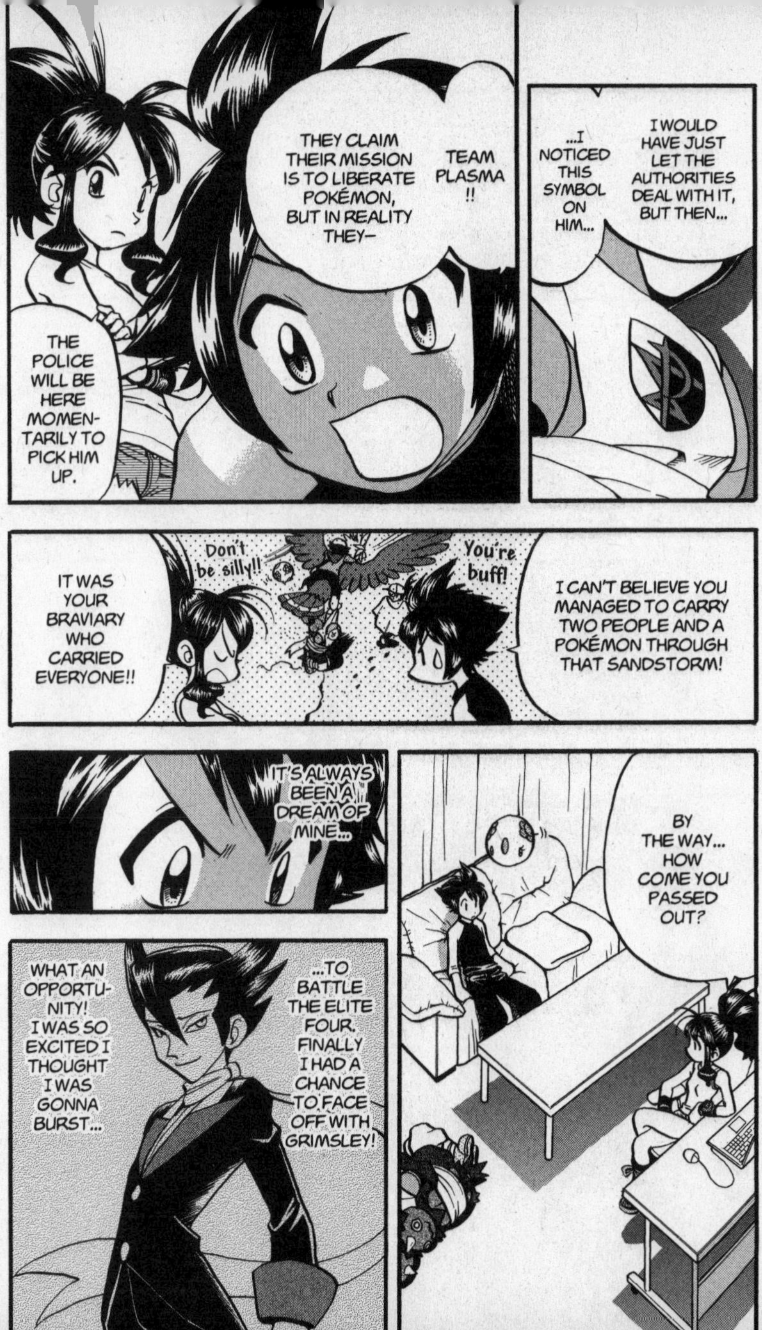
THE POLICE WILL BE HERE MOMENTARILY TO PICK HIM UP.
TEAM PLASMA!!
THEY CLAIM THEIR MISSION IS TO LIBERATE POKÉMON, BUT IN REALITY THEY–
...I NOTICED THIS SYMBOL ON HIM...
I WOULD HAVE JUST LET THE AUTHORITIES DEAL WITH IT, BUT THEN...
I CAN'T BELIEVE YOU MANAGED TO CARRY TWO PEOPLE AND A POKÉMON THROUGH THAT SANDSTORM!
IT WAS YOUR BRAVIARY WHO CARRIED EVERYONE!!
You're buff!
Don't be silly!!
BY THE WAY... HOW COME YOU PASSED OUT?
IT'S ALWAYS BEEN A DREAM OF MINE...
...TO BATTLE THE ELITE FOUR. FINALLY I HAD A CHANCE TO FACE OFF WITH GRIMSLEY!
WHAT AN OPPORTUNITY! I WAS SO EXCITED I THOUGHT I WAS GONNA BURST...

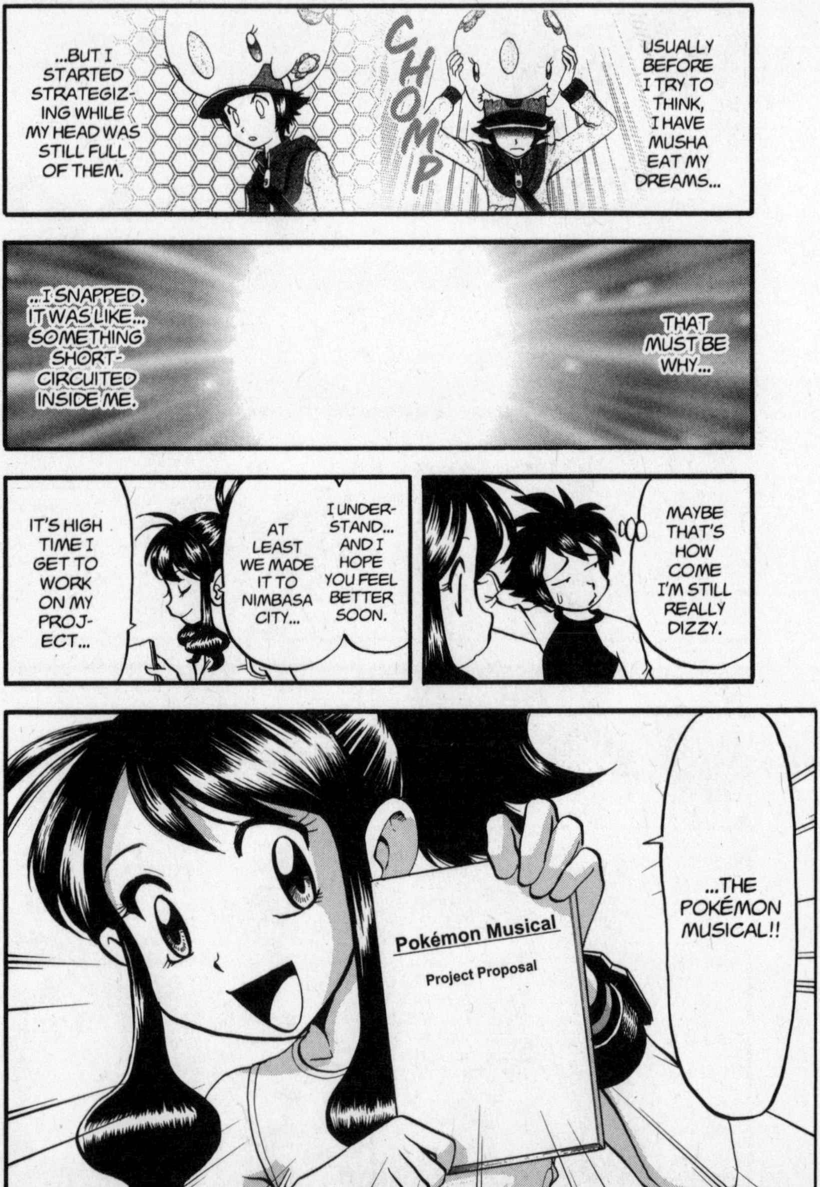
USUALLY BEFORE I TRY TO THINK, I HAVE MUSHA EAT MY DREAMS...
CHOMP
...BUT I STARTED STRATEGIZING WHILE MY HEAD WAS STILL FULL OF THEM.
THAT MUST BE WHY...
...I SNAPPED. IT WAS LIKE... SOMETHING SHORT-CIRCUITED INSIDE ME.
MAYBE THAT'S HOW COME I'M STILL REALLY DIZZY.
I UNDERSTAND... AND I HOPE YOU FEEL BETTER SOON.
AT LEAST WE MADE IT TO NIMBASA CITY...
IT'S HIGH TIME I GET TO WORK ON MY PROJECT...
...THE POKÉMON MUSICAL!!
Pokémon Musical
Project Proposal

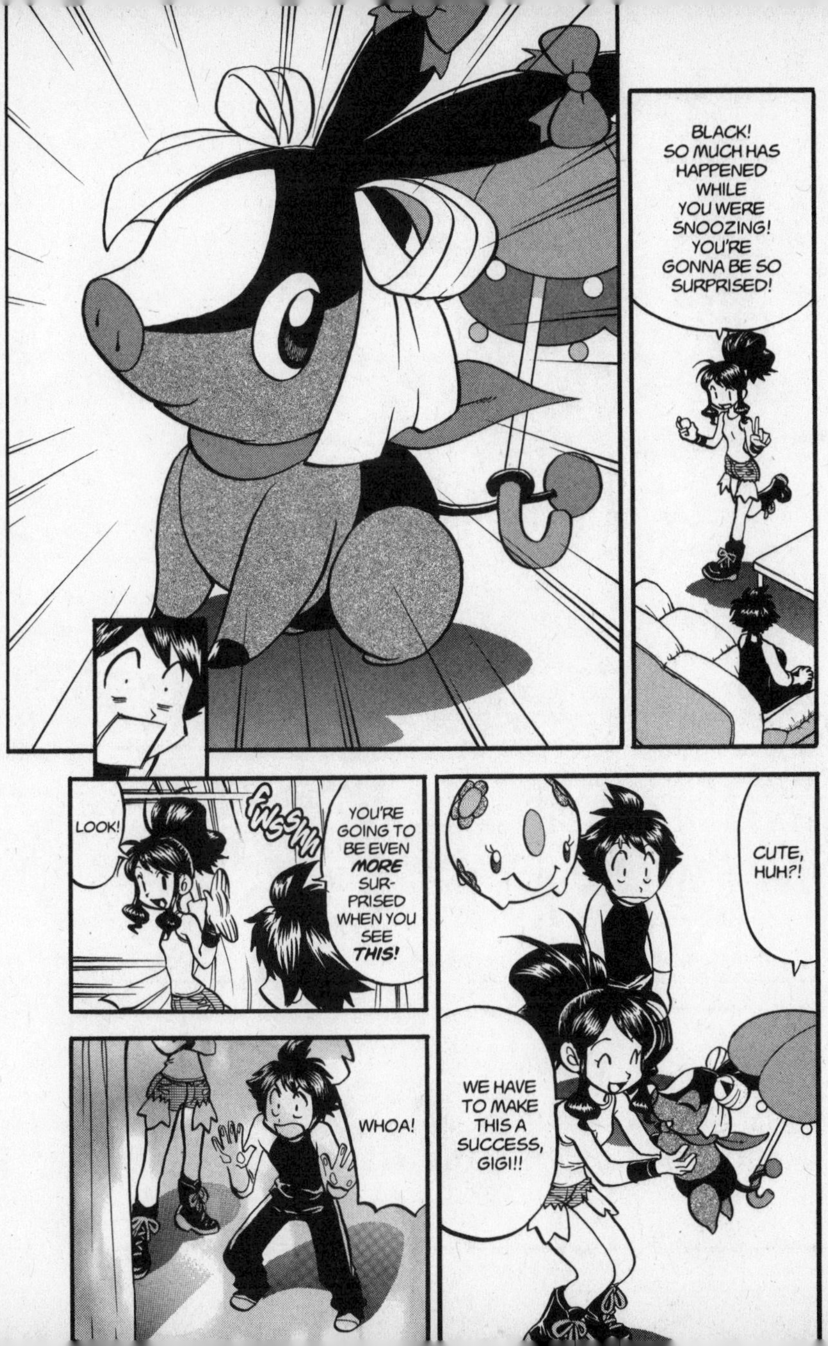
BLACK! SO MUCH HAS HAPPENED WHILE YOU WERE SNOOZING! YOU'RE GONNA BE SO SURPRISED!
LOOK!
FWSSHH
YOU'RE GOING TO BE EVEN MORE SUR-PRISED WHEN YOU SEE THIS!
CUTE, HUH?!
WHOA!
WE HAVE TO MAKE THIS A SUCCESS, GIGI!!

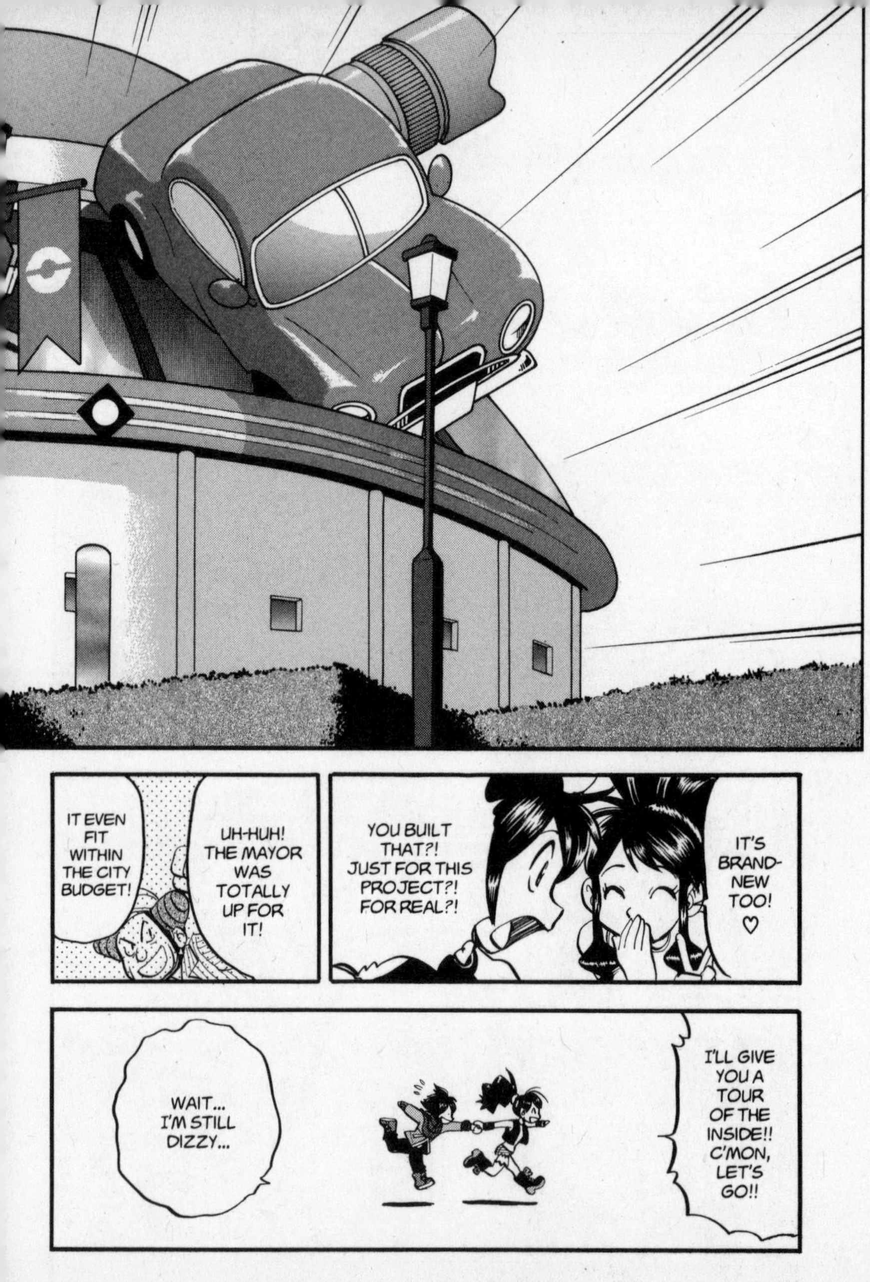

IT'S BRAND-NEW TOO! ♡
YOU BUILT THAT?! JUST FOR THIS PROJECT?! FOR REAL?!
UH-HUH! THE MAYOR WAS TOTALLY UP FOR IT!
IT EVEN FIT WITHIN THE CITY BUDGET!
I'LL GIVE YOU A TOUR OF THE INSIDE!! C'MON, LET'S GO!!
WAIT... I'M STILL DIZZY...

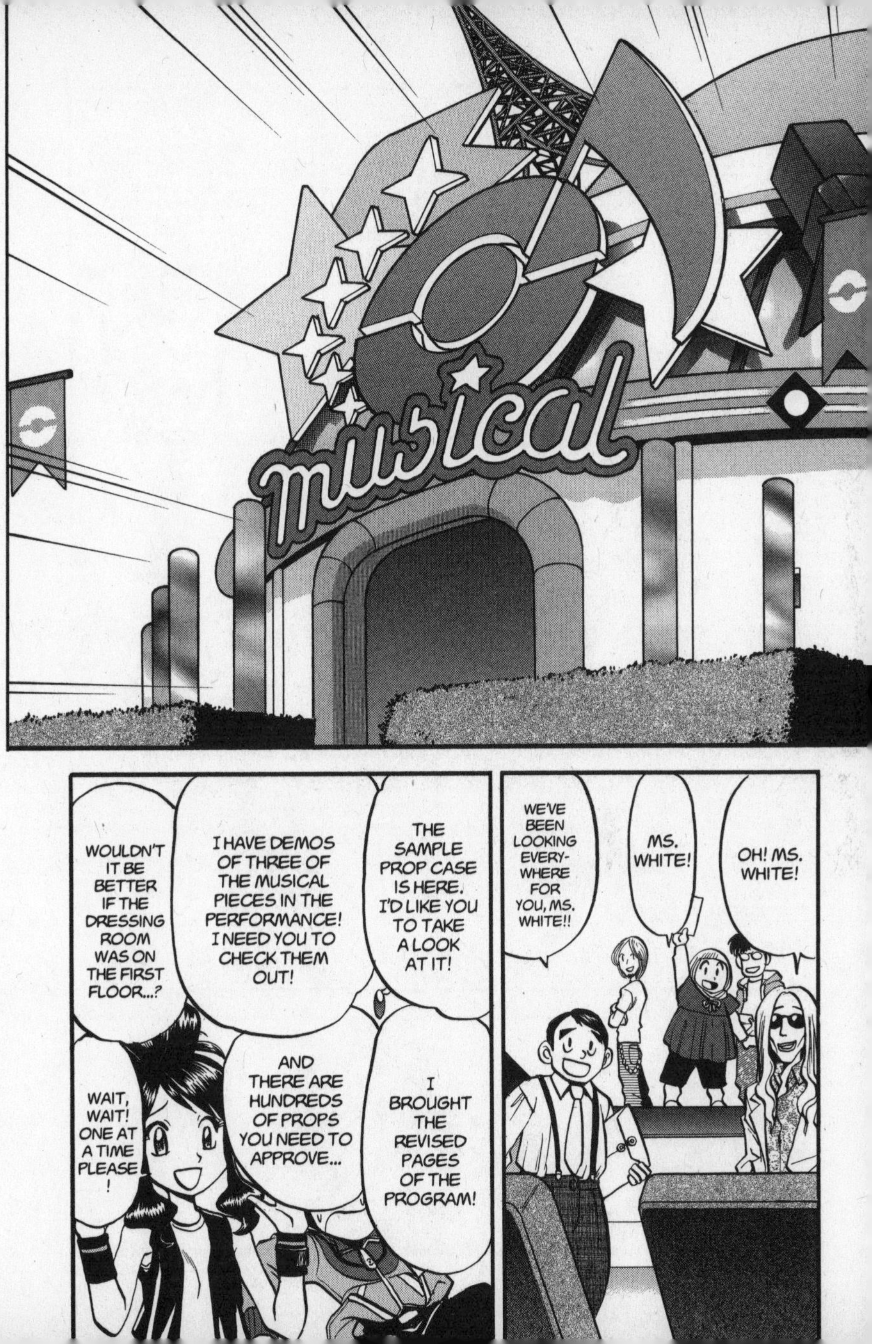
musical
OH! MS. WHITE!
MS. WHITE!
WE'VE BEEN LOOKING EVERY-WHERE FOR YOU, MS. WHITE!!
THE SAMPLE PROP CASE IS HERE. I'D LIKE YOU TO TAKE A LOOK AT IT!
I HAVE DEMOS OF THREE OF THE MUSICAL PIECES IN THE PERFORMANCE! I NEED YOU TO CHECK THEM OUT!
WOULDN'T IT BE BETTER IF THE DRESSING ROOM WAS ON THE FIRST FLOOR...?
I BROUGHT THE REVISED PAGES OF THE PROGRAM!
AND THERE ARE HUNDREDS OF PROPS YOU NEED TO APPROVE...
WAIT, WAIT! ONE AT A TIME PLEASE!

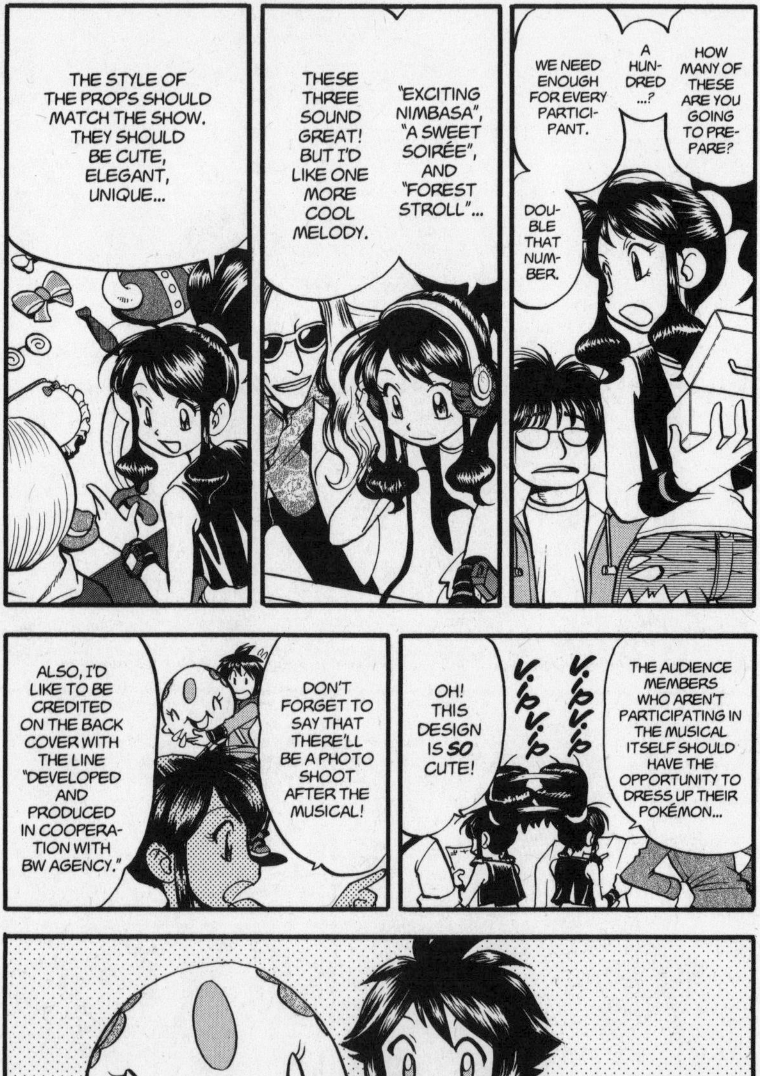
HOW MANY OF THESE ARE YOU GOING TO PREPARE?
A HUNDRED ...?
WE NEED ENOUGH FOR EVERY PARTICIPANT.
DOUBLE THAT NUMBER.
"EXCITING NIMBASA", "A SWEET SOIRÉE", AND "FOREST STROLL"...
THESE THREE SOUND GREAT! BUT I'D LIKE ONE MORE COOL MELODY.
THE STYLE OF THE PROPS SHOULD MATCH THE SHOW. THEY SHOULD BE CUTE, ELEGANT, UNIQUE...
THE AUDIENCE MEMBERS WHO AREN'T PARTICIPATING IN THE MUSICAL ITSELF SHOULD HAVE THE OPPORTUNITY TO DRESS UP THEIR POKÉMON...
V.i.p V.i.p
V.i.p V.i.p
OH! THIS DESIGN IS **SO** CUTE!
DON'T FORGET TO SAY THAT THERE'LL BE A PHOTO SHOOT AFTER THE MUSICAL!
ALSO, I'D LIKE TO BE CREDITED ON THE BACK COVER WITH THE LINE "DEVELOPED AND PRODUCED IN COOPERATION WITH BW AGENCY."

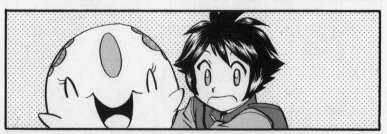

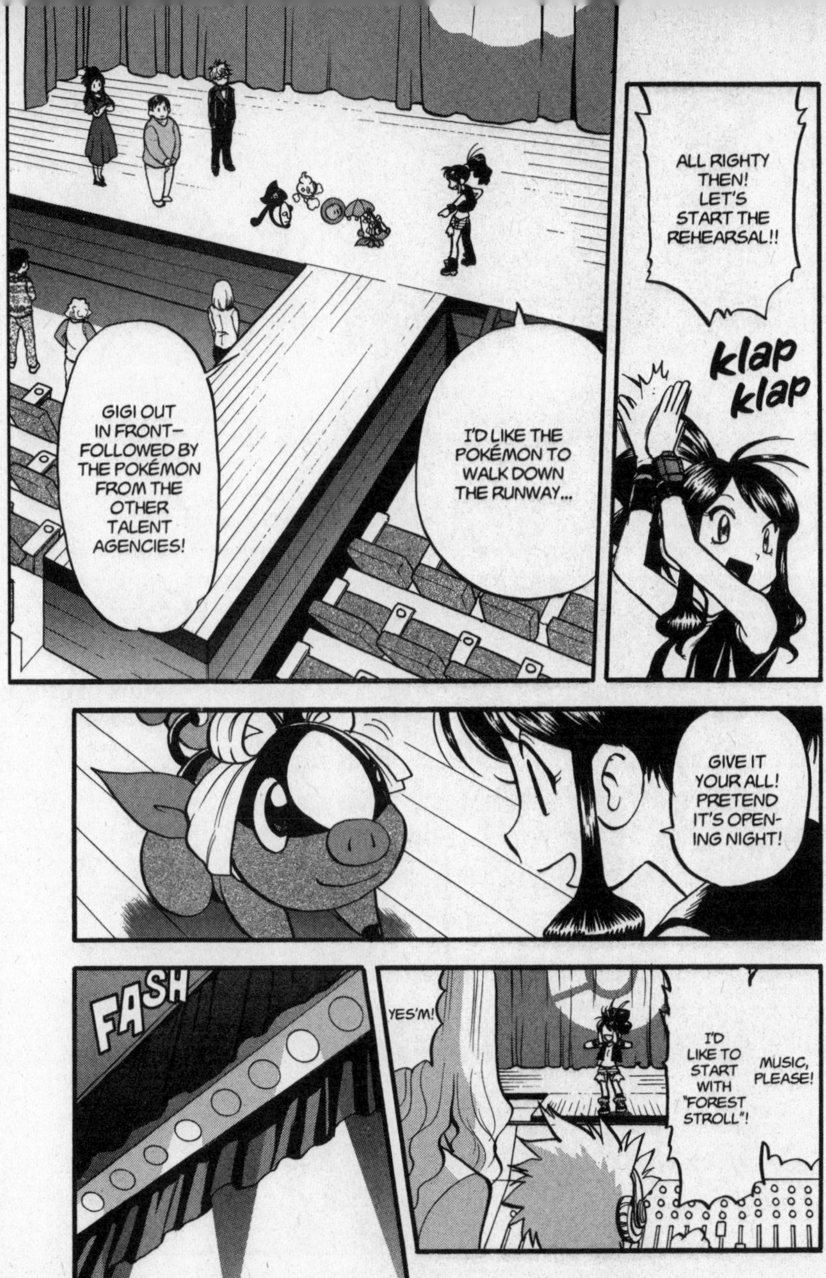

ALL RIGHTY THEN! LET'S START THE REHEARSAL!!
klap klap
I'D LIKE THE POKÉMON TO WALK DOWN THE RUNWAY...
GIGI OUT IN FRONT—FOLLOWED BY THE POKÉMON FROM THE OTHER TALENT AGENCIES!
GIVE IT YOUR ALL! PRETEND IT'S OPEN-ING NIGHT!
FASH
YES'M!
I'D LIKE TO START WITH "FOREST STROLL"!
MUSIC, PLEASE!

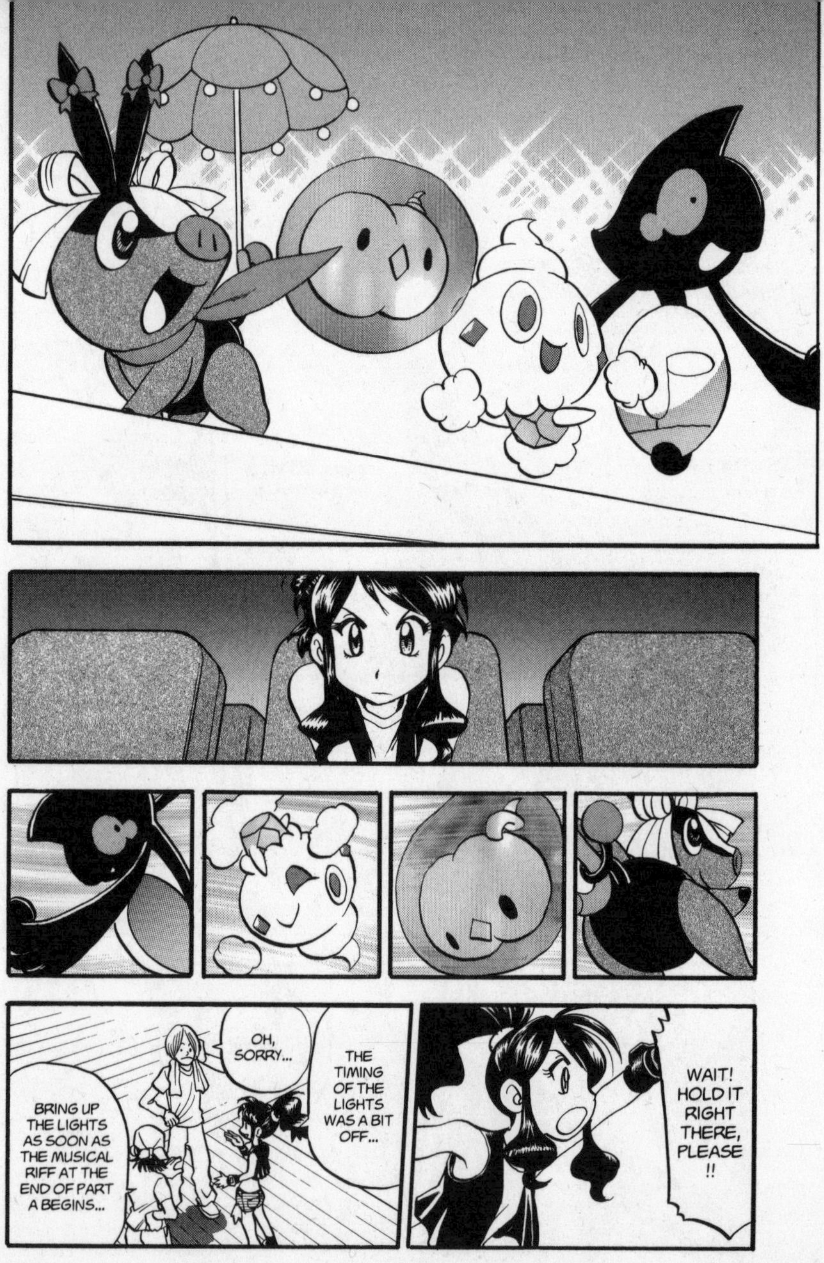
WAIT! HOLD IT RIGHT THERE, PLEASE!!
THE TIMING OF THE LIGHTS WAS A BIT OFF...
OH, SORRY...
BRING UP THE LIGHTS AS SOON AS THE MUSICAL RIFF AT THE END OF PART A BEGINS...

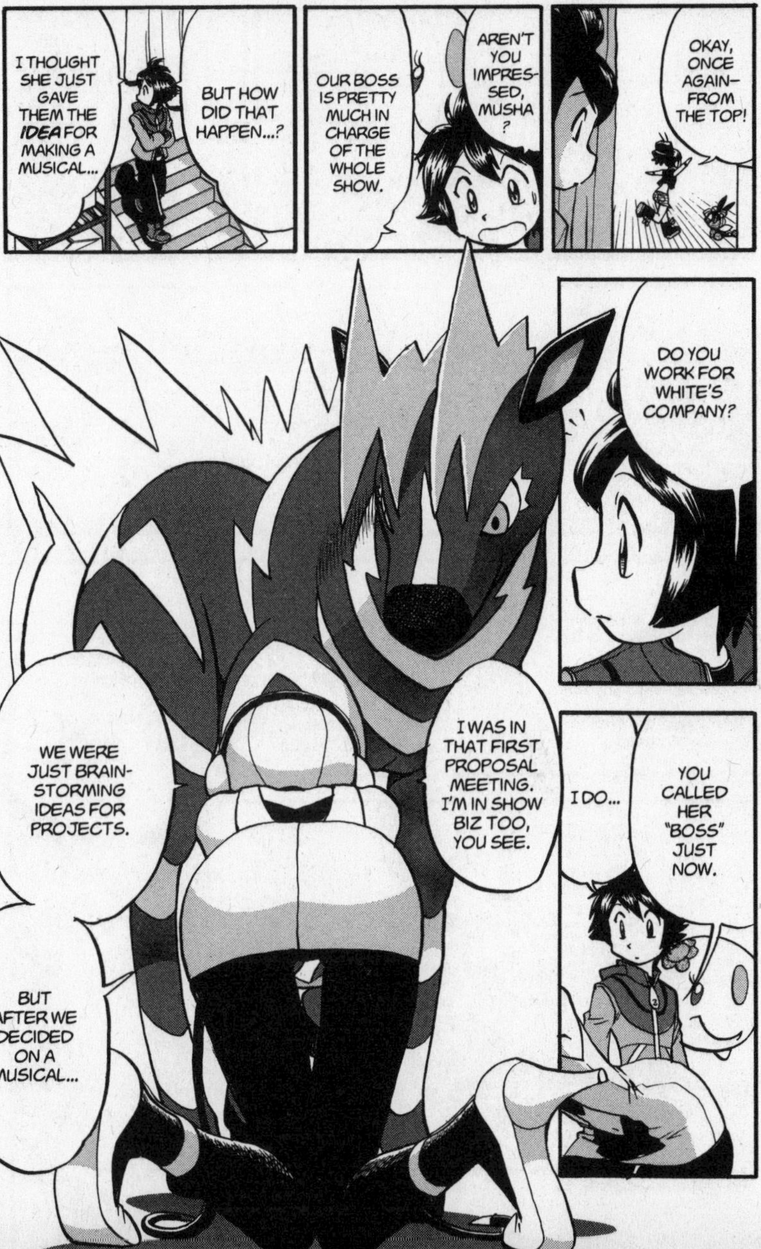
I THOUGHT SHE JUST GAVE THEM THE IDEA FOR MAKING A MUSICAL...
BUT HOW DID THAT HAPPEN...?
OUR BOSS IS PRETTY MUCH IN CHARGE OF THE WHOLE SHOW.
AREN'T YOU IMPRES-SED, MUSHA?
OKAY, ONCE AGAIN—FROM THE TOP!
DO YOU WORK FOR WHITE'S COMPANY?
I DO...
YOU CALLED HER "BOSS" JUST NOW.
I WAS IN THAT FIRST PROPOSAL MEETING. I'M IN SHOW BIZ TOO, YOU SEE.
WE WERE JUST BRAIN-STORMING IDEAS FOR PROJECTS.
BUT AFTER WE DECIDED ON A MUSICAL...

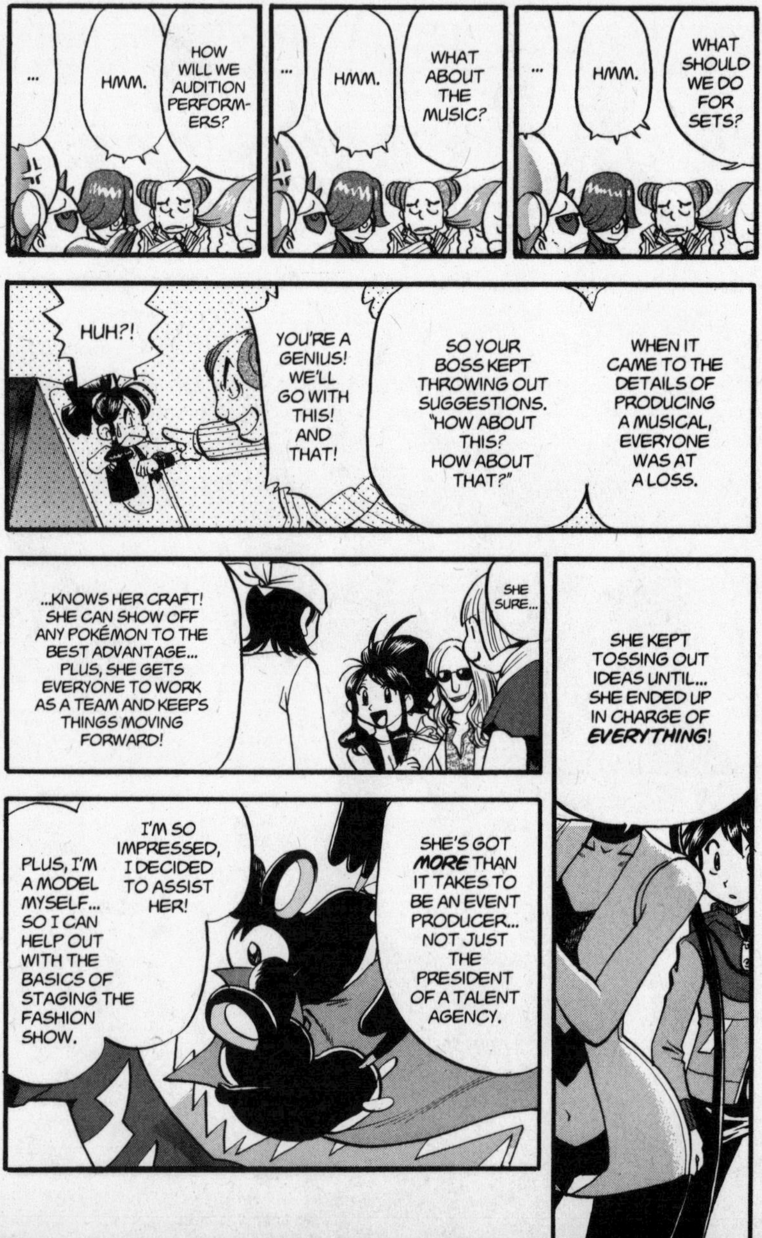
HOW WILL WE AUDITION PERFORMERS?
HMM.
...
WHAT ABOUT THE MUSIC?
HMM.
...
WHAT SHOULD WE DO FOR SETS?
HMM.
...
WHEN IT CAME TO THE DETAILS OF PRODUCING A MUSICAL, EVERYONE WAS AT A LOSS.
SO YOUR BOSS KEPT THROWING OUT SUGGESTIONS. "HOW ABOUT THIS? HOW ABOUT THAT?"
YOU'RE A GENIUS! WE'LL GO WITH THIS! AND THAT!
HUH?!
SHE KEPT TOSSING OUT IDEAS UNTIL... SHE ENDED UP IN CHARGE OF *EVERYTHING*!
SHE SURE...
...KNOWS HER CRAFT! SHE CAN SHOW OFF ANY POKÉMON TO THE BEST ADVANTAGE... PLUS, SHE GETS EVERYONE TO WORK AS A TEAM AND KEEPS THINGS MOVING FORWARD!
SHE'S GOT *MORE* THAN IT TAKES TO BE AN EVENT PRODUCER... NOT JUST THE PRESIDENT OF A TALENT AGENCY.
I'M SO IMPRESSED, I DECIDED TO ASSIST HER!
PLUS, I'M A MODEL MYSELF... SO I CAN HELP OUT WITH THE BASICS OF STAGING THE FASHION SHOW.

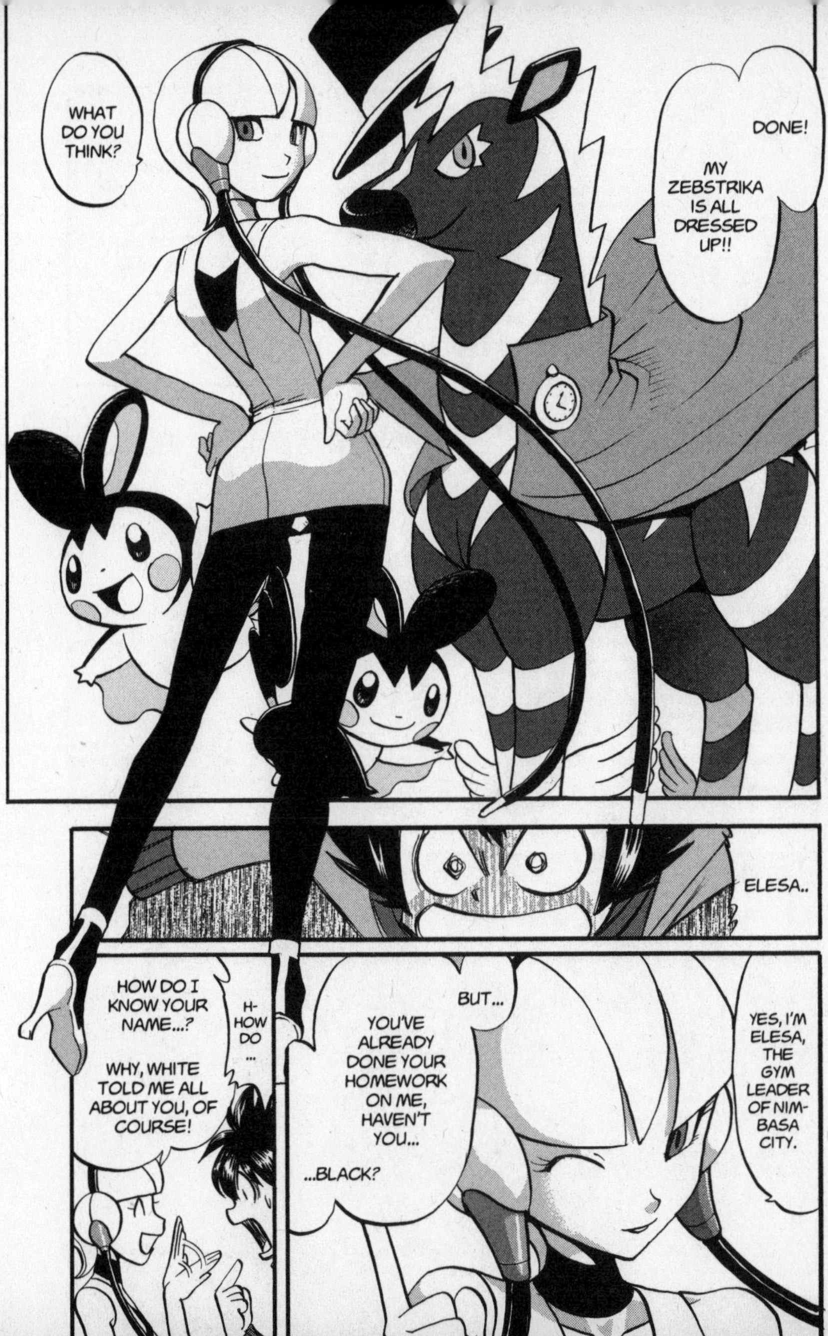

DONE!
MY ZEBSTRIKA IS ALL DRESSED UP!!
WHAT DO YOU THINK?
ELESA..
YES, I'M ELESA, THE GYM LEADER OF NIM-BASA CITY.
BUT...
YOU'VE ALREADY DONE YOUR HOMEWORK ON ME, HAVEN'T YOU...
...BLACK?
H-HOW DO ...
HOW DO I KNOW YOUR NAME...?
WHY, WHITE TOLD ME ALL ABOUT YOU, OF COURSE!

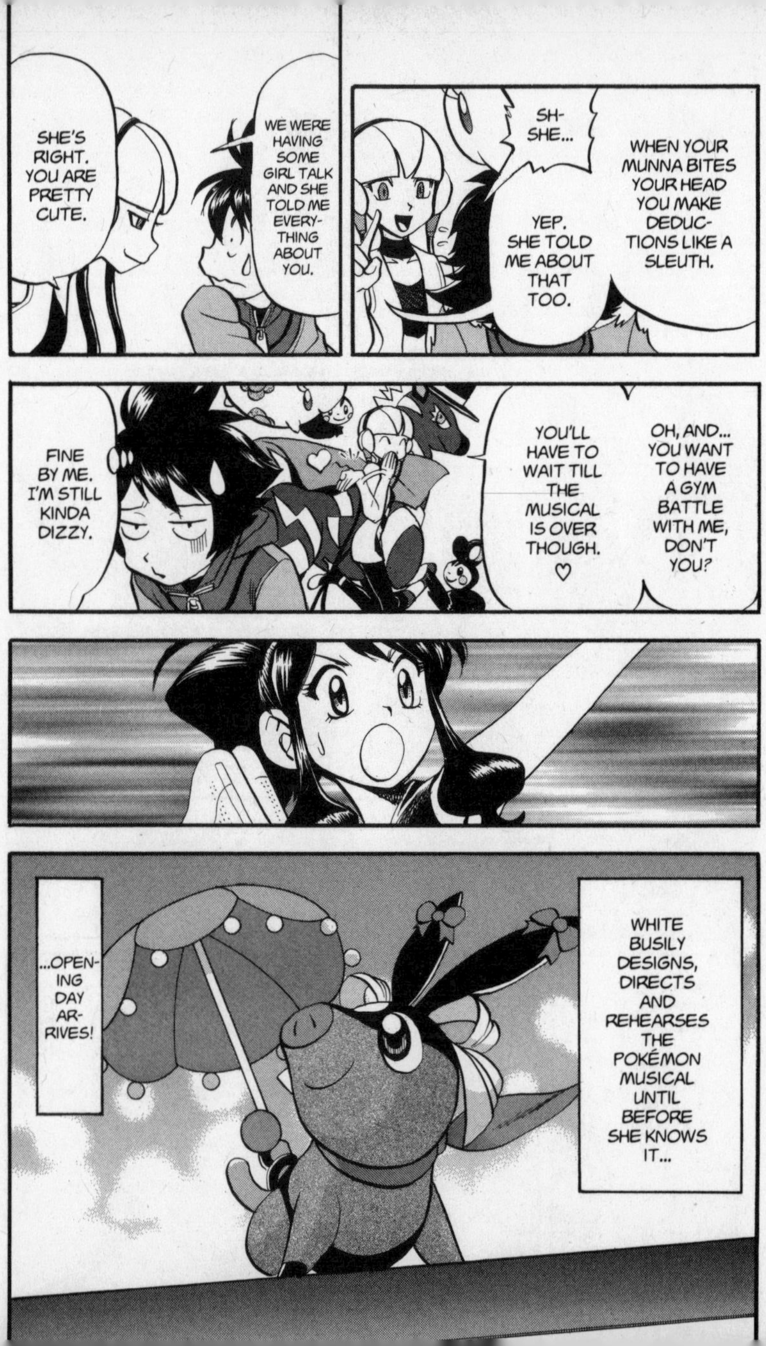
SHE'S RIGHT. YOU ARE PRETTY CUTE.
WE WERE HAVING SOME GIRL TALK AND SHE TOLD ME EVERY-THING ABOUT YOU.
SH- SHE...
WHEN YOUR MUNNA BITES YOUR HEAD YOU MAKE DEDUC-TIONS LIKE A SLEUTH.
YEP. SHE TOLD ME ABOUT THAT TOO.
OH, AND... YOU WANT TO HAVE A GYM BATTLE WITH ME, DON'T YOU?
YOU'LL HAVE TO WAIT TILL THE MUSICAL IS OVER THOUGH. ♡
FINE BY ME. I'M STILL KINDA DIZZY.
WHITE BUSILY DESIGNS, DIRECTS AND REHEARSES THE POKÉMON MUSICAL UNTIL BEFORE SHE KNOWS IT...
...OPEN-ING DAY AR-RIVES!

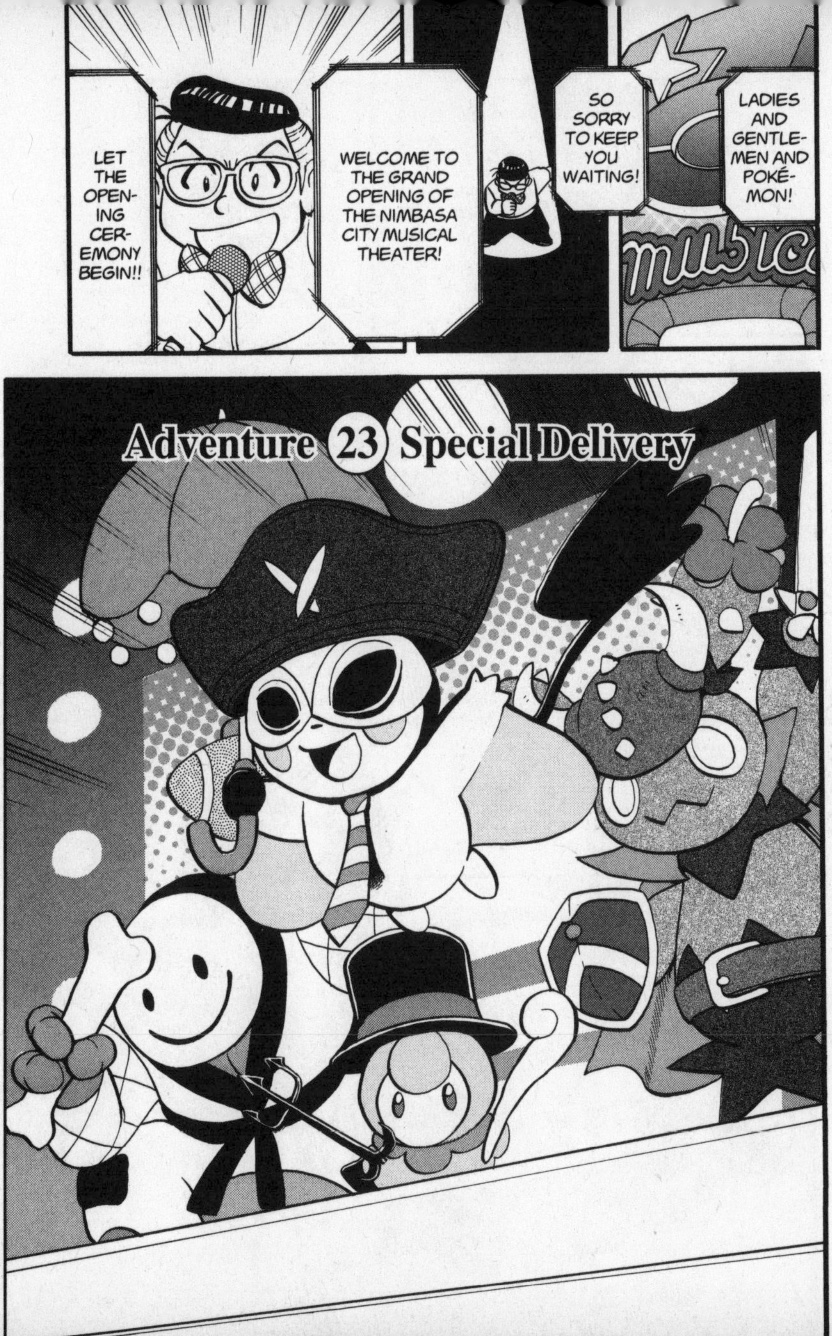
LADIES AND GENTLEMEN AND POKÉMON!
SO SORRY TO KEEP YOU WAITING!
WELCOME TO THE GRAND OPENING OF THE NIMBASA CITY MUSICAL THEATER!
LET THE OPENING CEREMONY BEGIN!!
Adventure 23 Special Delivery

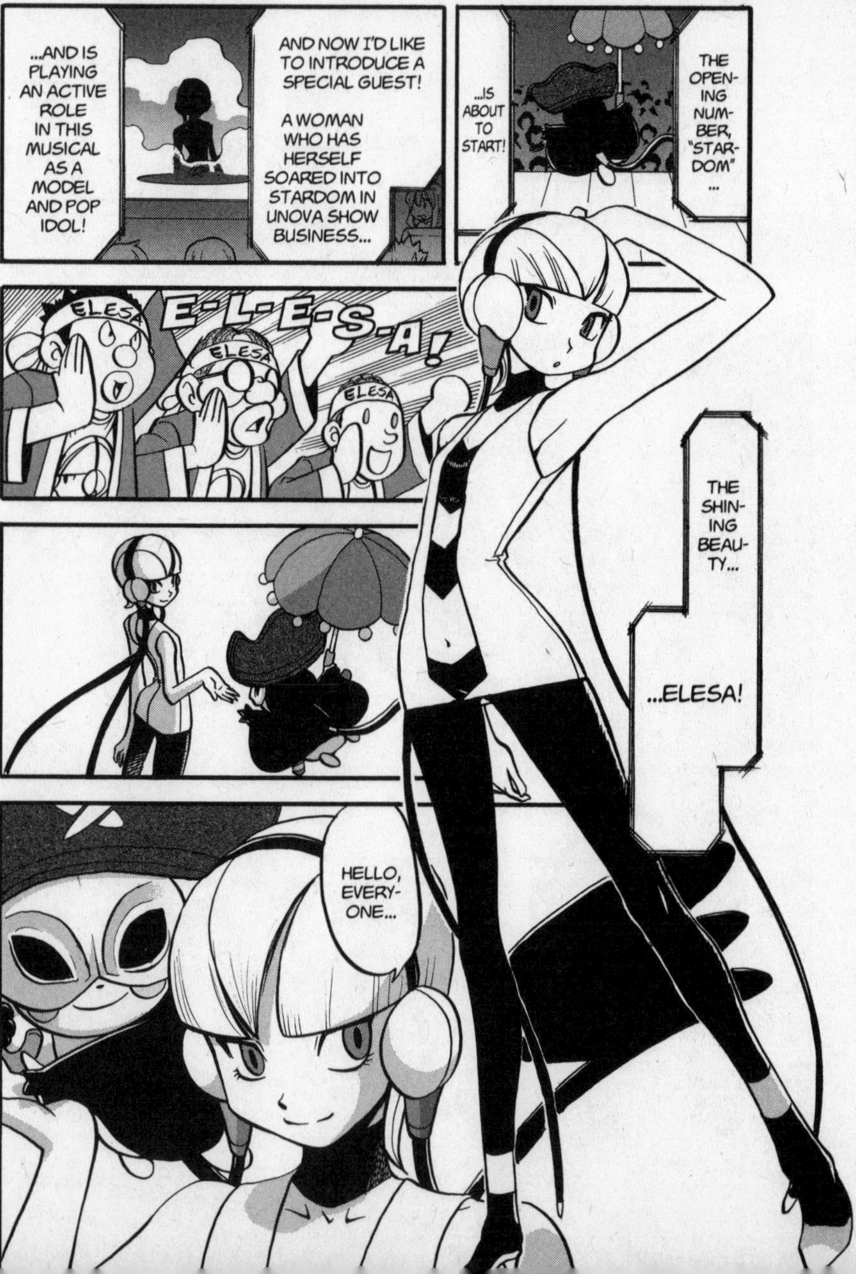
THE OPENING NUMBER, "STARDOM"...
...IS ABOUT TO START!
AND NOW I'D LIKE TO INTRODUCE A SPECIAL GUEST!
A WOMAN WHO HAS HERSELF SOARED INTO STARDOM IN UNOVA SHOW BUSINESS...
...AND IS PLAYING AN ACTIVE ROLE IN THIS MUSICAL AS A MODEL AND POP IDOL!
ELESA
ELESA
ELESA
E-L-E-S-A!
THE SHINING BEAUTY...
...ELESA!
HELLO, EVERYONE...

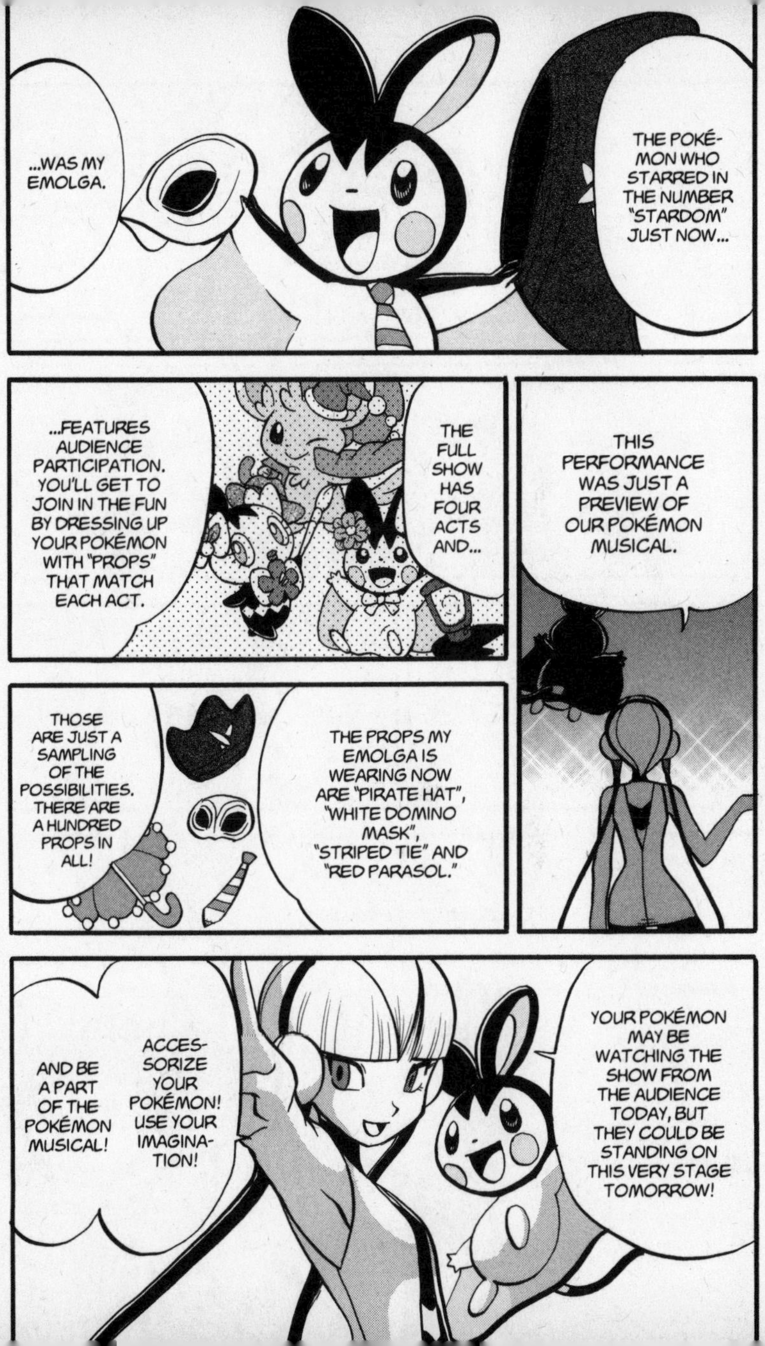
THE POKÉMON WHO STARRED IN THE NUMBER "STARDOM" JUST NOW...
...WAS MY EMOLGA.
THIS PERFORMANCE WAS JUST A PREVIEW OF OUR POKÉMON MUSICAL.
THE FULL SHOW HAS FOUR ACTS AND...
...FEATURES AUDIENCE PARTICIPATION. YOU'LL GET TO JOIN IN THE FUN BY DRESSING UP YOUR POKÉMON WITH "PROPS" THAT MATCH EACH ACT.
THE PROPS MY EMOLGA IS WEARING NOW ARE "PIRATE HAT", "WHITE DOMINO MASK", "STRIPED TIE" AND "RED PARASOL."
THOSE ARE JUST A SAMPLING OF THE POSSIBILITIES. THERE ARE A HUNDRED PROPS IN ALL!
YOUR POKÉMON MAY BE WATCHING THE SHOW FROM THE AUDIENCE TODAY, BUT THEY COULD BE STANDING ON THIS VERY STAGE TOMORROW!
ACCES-SORIZE YOUR POKÉMON! USE YOUR IMAGINA-TION!
AND BE A PART OF THE POKÉMON MUSICAL!

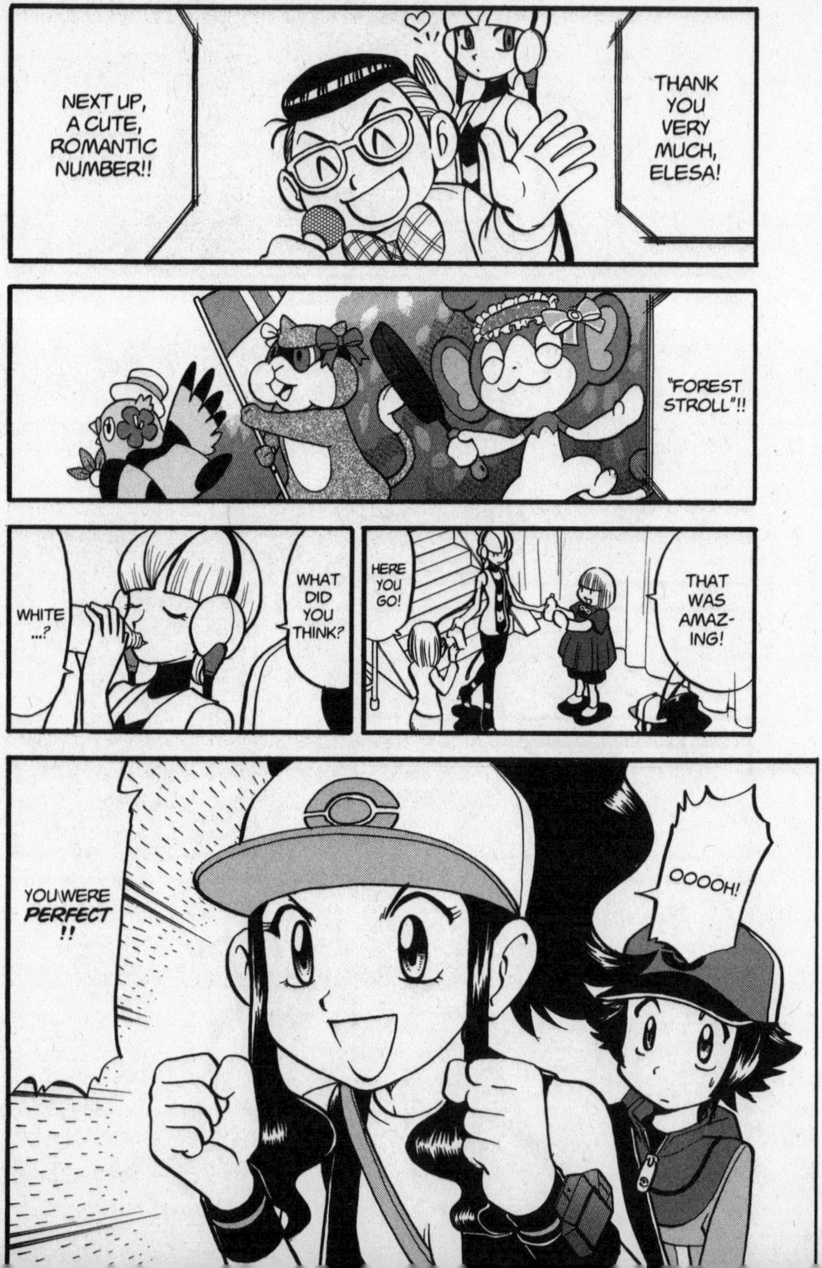
NEXT UP, A CUTE, ROMANTIC NUMBER!!
THANK YOU VERY MUCH, ELESA!
"FOREST STROLL"!!
WHITE ...?
WHAT DID YOU THINK?
HERE YOU GO!
THAT WAS AMAZ-ING!
YOU WERE PERFECT!!
OOOOH!

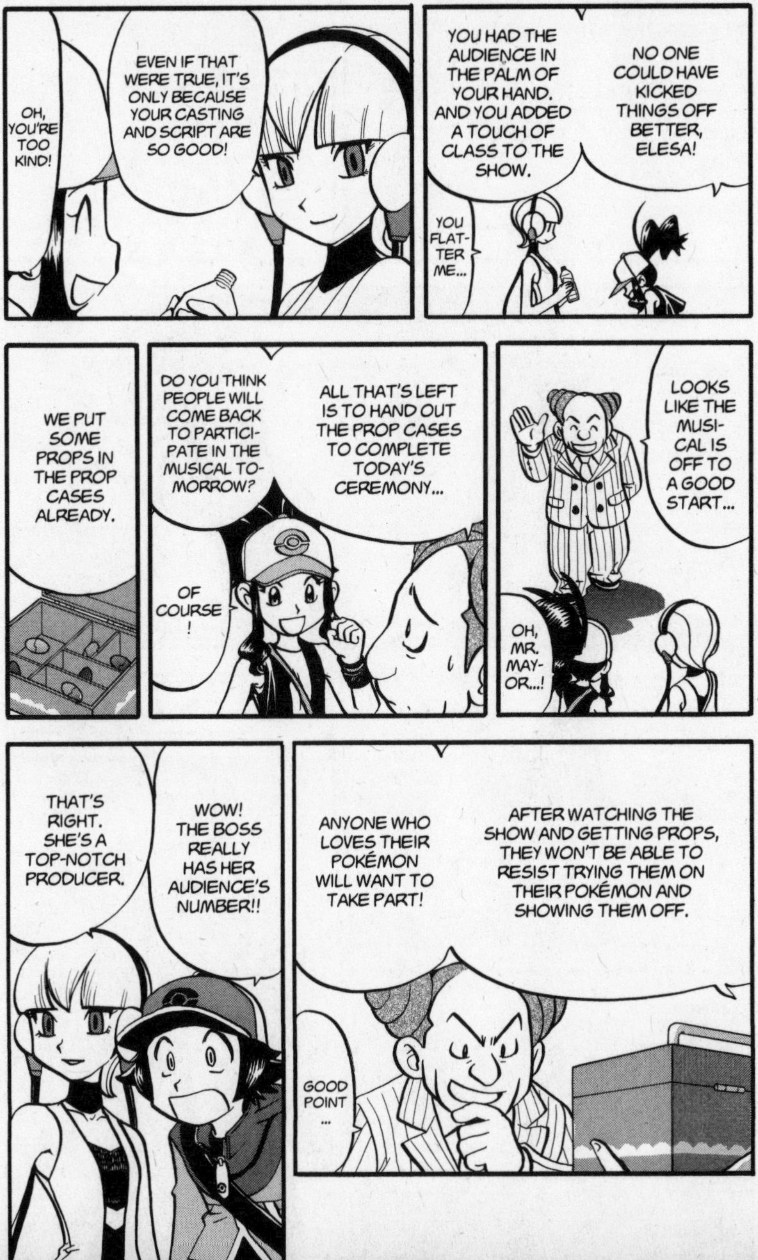
OH, YOU'RE TOO KIND!
EVEN IF THAT WERE TRUE, IT'S ONLY BECAUSE YOUR CASTING AND SCRIPT ARE SO GOOD!
YOU HAD THE AUDIENCE IN THE PALM OF YOUR HAND. AND YOU ADDED A TOUCH OF CLASS TO THE SHOW.
NO ONE COULD HAVE KICKED THINGS OFF BETTER, ELESA!
YOU FLATTER ME...
WE PUT SOME PROPS IN THE PROP CASES ALREADY.
DO YOU THINK PEOPLE WILL COME BACK TO PARTICIPATE IN THE MUSICAL TOMORROW?
ALL THAT'S LEFT IS TO HAND OUT THE PROP CASES TO COMPLETE TODAY'S CEREMONY...
OF COURSE!
LOOKS LIKE THE MUSICAL IS OFF TO A GOOD START...
OH, MR. MAYOR...!
THAT'S RIGHT. SHE'S A TOP-NOTCH PRODUCER.
WOW! THE BOSS REALLY HAS HER AUDIENCE'S NUMBER!!
ANYONE WHO LOVES THEIR POKÉMON WILL WANT TO TAKE PART!
AFTER WATCHING THE SHOW AND GETTING PROPS, THEY WON'T BE ABLE TO RESIST TRYING THEM ON THEIR POKÉMON AND SHOWING THEM OFF.
GOOD POINT...

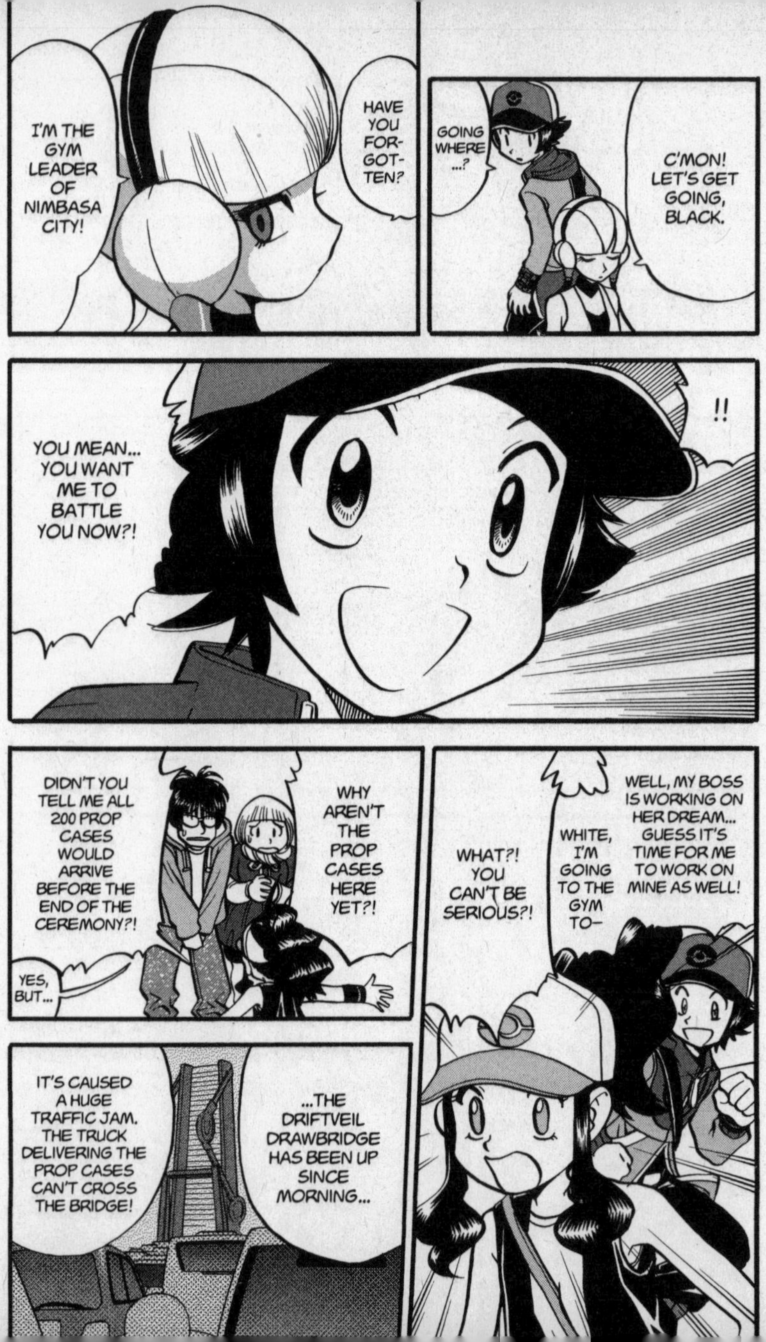

I'M THE GYM LEADER OF NIMBASA CITY!
HAVE YOU FOR-GOT-TEN?
GOING WHERE ...?
C'MON! LET'S GET GOING, BLACK.
YOU MEAN... YOU WANT ME TO BATTLE YOU NOW?!
!!
DIDN'T YOU TELL ME ALL 200 PROP CASES WOULD ARRIVE BEFORE THE END OF THE CEREMONY?!
WHY AREN'T THE PROP CASES HERE YET?!
YES, BUT...
WHAT?! YOU CAN'T BE SERIOUS?!
WHITE, I'M GOING TO THE GYM TO—
WELL, MY BOSS IS WORKING ON HER DREAM... GUESS IT'S TIME FOR ME TO WORK ON MINE AS WELL!
IT'S CAUSED A HUGE TRAFFIC JAM. THE TRUCK DELIVERING THE PROP CASES CAN'T CROSS THE BRIDGE!
...THE DRIFTVEIL DRAWBRIDGE HAS BEEN UP SINCE MORNING...

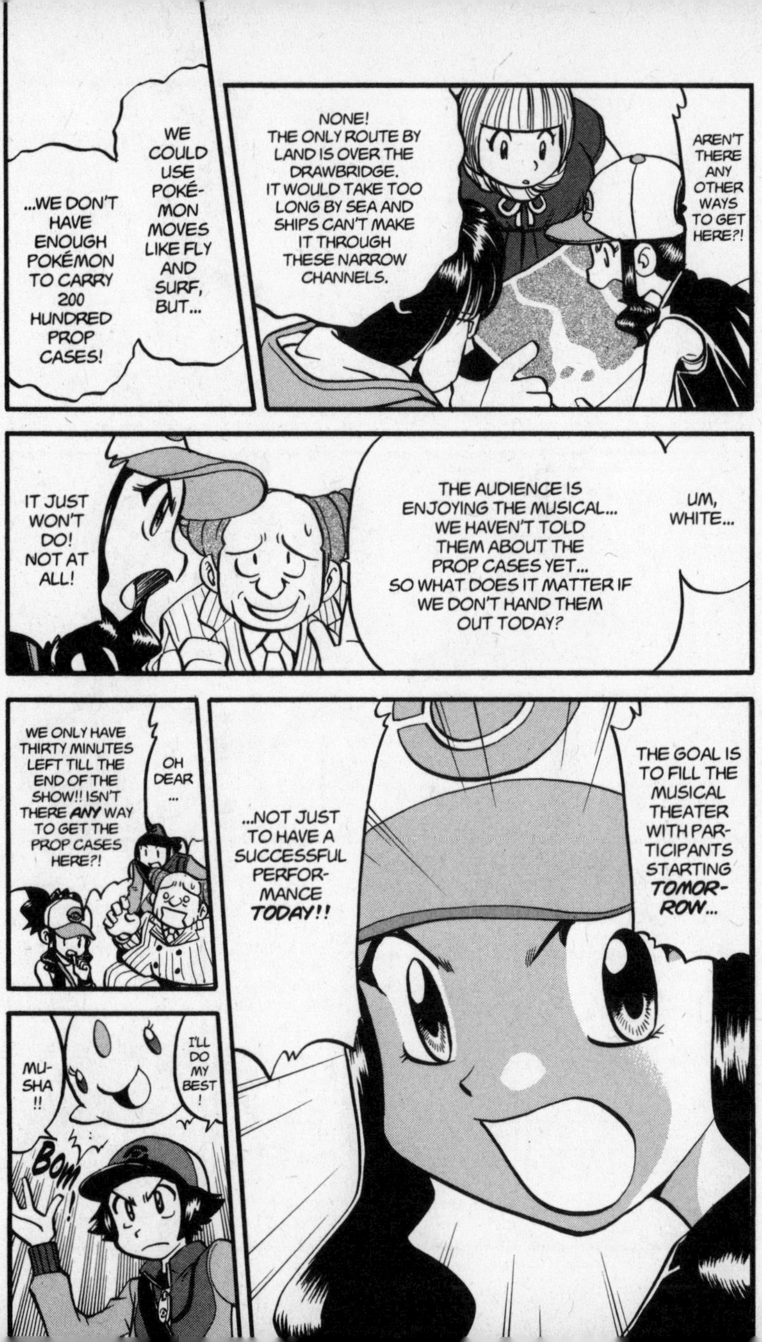
AREN'T THERE ANY OTHER WAYS TO GET HERE?!
NONE! THE ONLY ROUTE BY LAND IS OVER THE DRAWBRIDGE. IT WOULD TAKE TOO LONG BY SEA AND SHIPS CAN'T MAKE IT THROUGH THESE NARROW CHANNELS.
WE COULD USE POKÉMON MOVES LIKE FLY AND SURF, BUT...
...WE DON'T HAVE ENOUGH POKÉMON TO CARRY 200 HUNDRED PROP CASES!
UM, WHITE...
THE AUDIENCE IS ENJOYING THE MUSICAL... WE HAVEN'T TOLD THEM ABOUT THE PROP CASES YET... SO WHAT DOES IT MATTER IF WE DON'T HAND THEM OUT TODAY?
IT JUST WON'T DO! NOT AT ALL!
THE GOAL IS TO FILL THE MUSICAL THEATER WITH PARTICIPANTS STARTING TOMORROW...
...NOT JUST TO HAVE A SUCCESSFUL PERFORMANCE TODAY!!
OH DEAR...
WE ONLY HAVE THIRTY MINUTES LEFT TILL THE END OF THE SHOW!! ISN'T THERE ANY WAY TO GET THE PROP CASES HERE?!
I'LL DO MY BEST!
MUSHA!!
BOM!

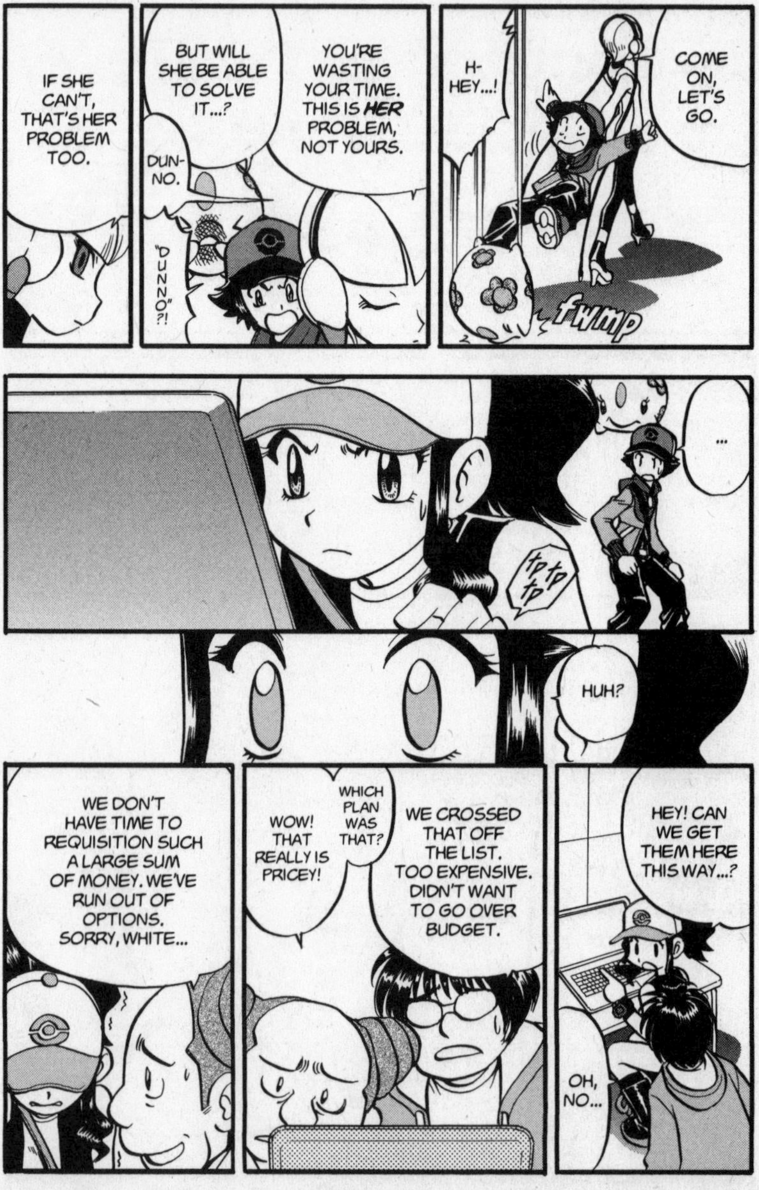
COME ON, LET'S GO.
H-HEY...!
fwmp
YOU'RE WASTING YOUR TIME. THIS IS HER PROBLEM, NOT YOURS.
BUT WILL SHE BE ABLE TO SOLVE IT...?
DUN-NO.
"DUNNO"?!
IF SHE CAN'T, THAT'S HER PROBLEM TOO.
...
tp tp tp
HUH?
HEY! CAN WE GET THEM HERE THIS WAY...?
OH, NO...
WE CROSSED THAT OFF THE LIST. TOO EXPENSIVE. DIDN'T WANT TO GO OVER BUDGET.
WHICH PLAN WAS THAT?
WOW! THAT REALLY IS PRICEY!
WE DON'T HAVE TIME TO REQUISITION SUCH A LARGE SUM OF MONEY. WE'VE RUN OUT OF OPTIONS. SORRY, WHITE...

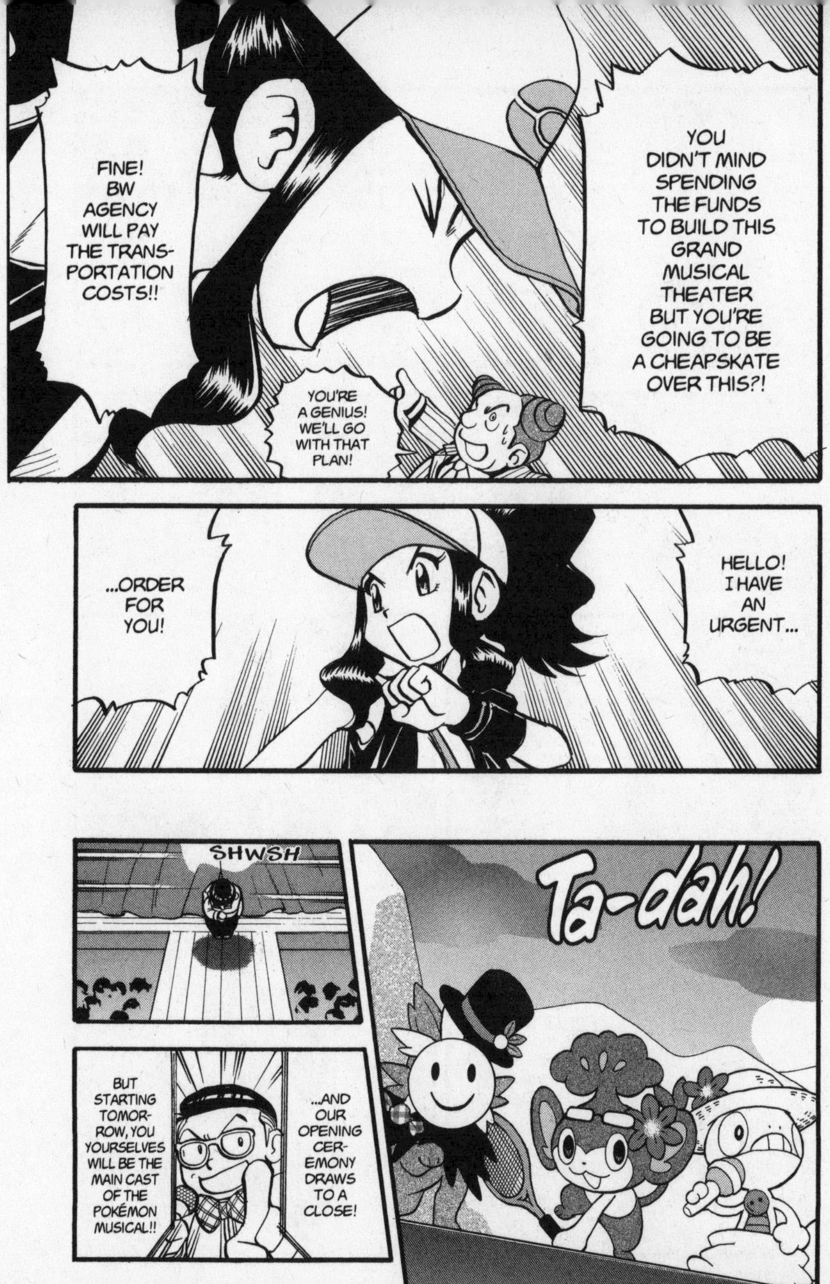
YOU DIDN'T MIND SPENDING THE FUNDS TO BUILD THIS GRAND MUSICAL THEATER BUT YOU'RE GOING TO BE A CHEAPSKATE OVER THIS?!
FINE! BW AGENCY WILL PAY THE TRANS-PORTATION COSTS!!
YOU'RE A GENIUS! WE'LL GO WITH THAT PLAN!
HELLO! I HAVE AN URGENT...
...ORDER FOR YOU!
SHWSH
Ta-dah!
...AND OUR OPENING CER-EMONY DRAWS TO A CLOSE!
BUT STARTING TOMOR-ROW, YOU YOURSELVES WILL BE THE MAIN CAST OF THE POKÉMON MUSICAL!!

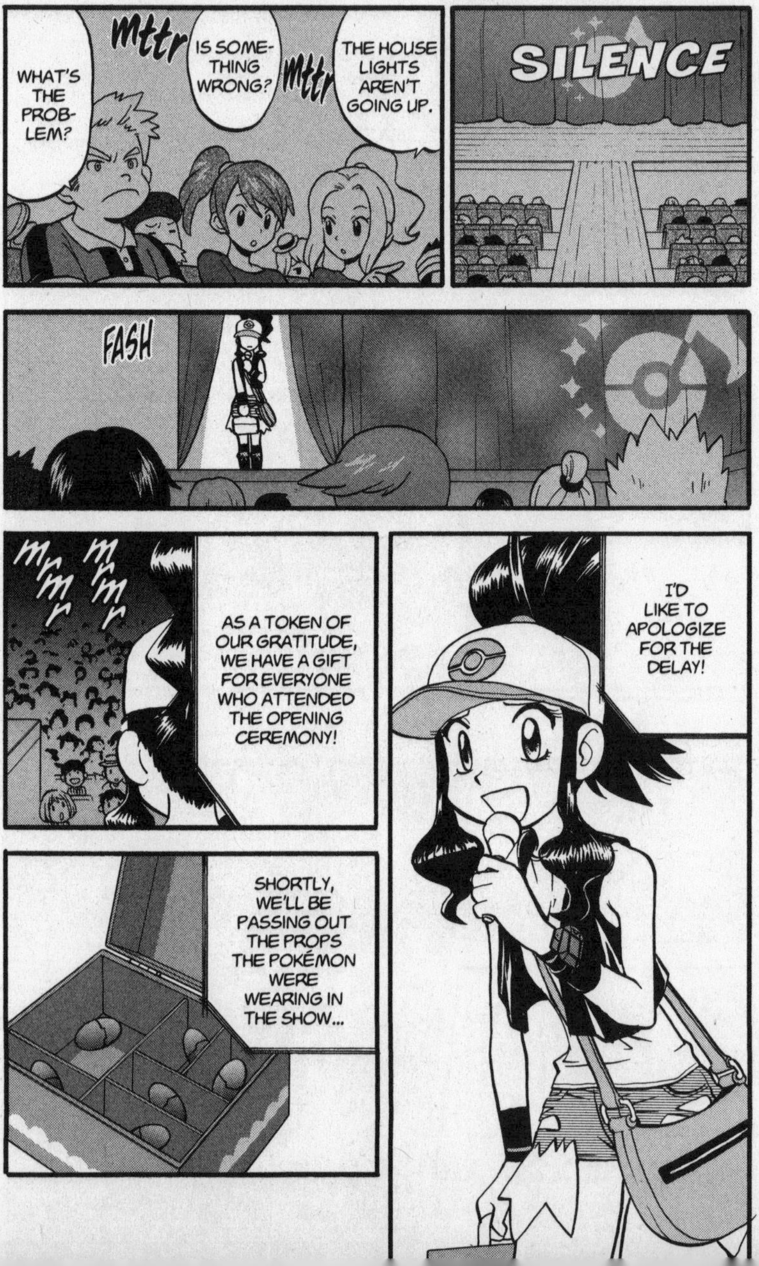
WHAT'S THE PROBLEM?
mttr
IS SOMETHING WRONG?
mttr
THE HOUSE LIGHTS AREN'T GOING UP.
SILENCE
FASH
mrmr
mrmr
I'D LIKE TO APOLOGIZE FOR THE DELAY!
AS A TOKEN OF OUR GRATITUDE, WE HAVE A GIFT FOR EVERYONE WHO ATTENDED THE OPENING CEREMONY!
SHORTLY, WE'LL BE PASSING OUT THE PROPS THE POKÉMON WERE WEARING IN THE SHOW...

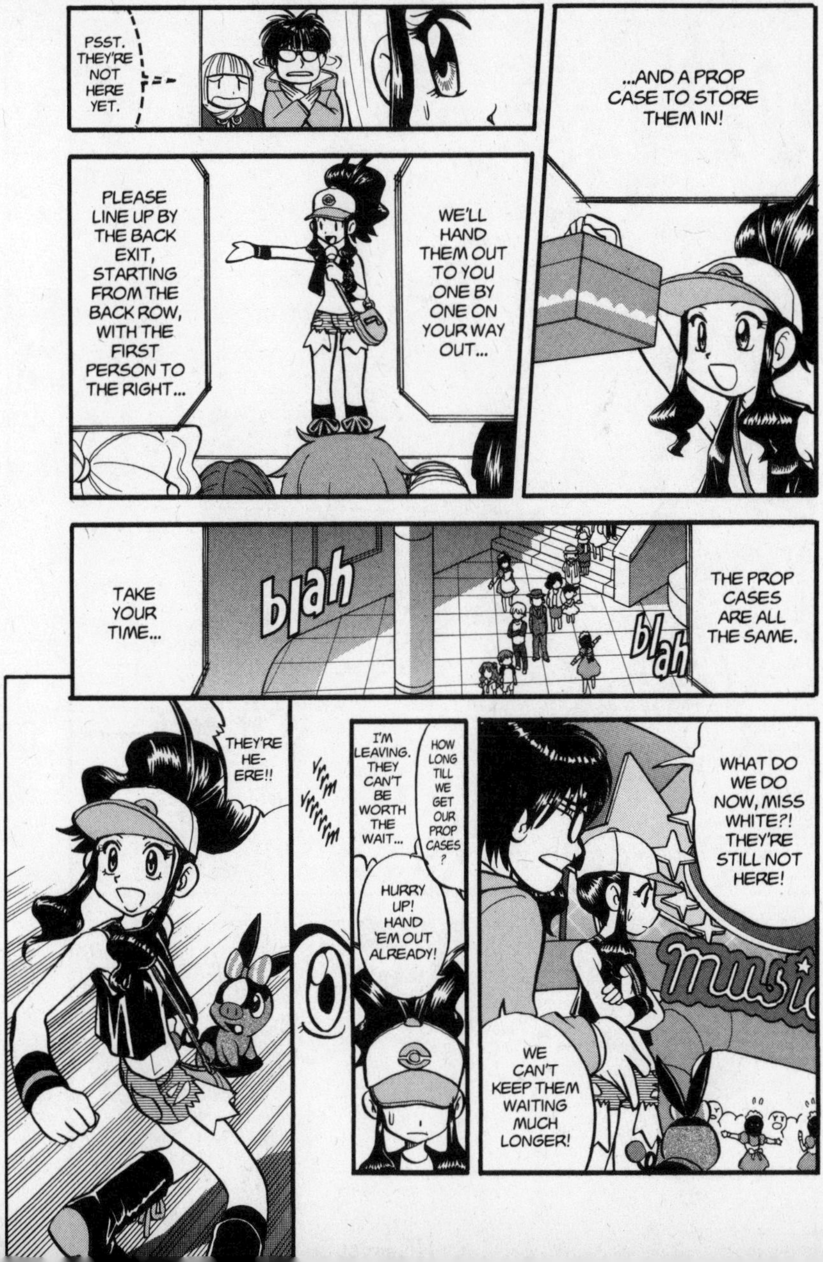
PSST. THEY'RE NOT HERE YET.
...AND A PROP CASE TO STORE THEM IN!
PLEASE LINE UP BY THE BACK EXIT, STARTING FROM THE BACK ROW, WITH THE FIRST PERSON TO THE RIGHT...
WE'LL HAND THEM OUT TO YOU ONE BY ONE ON YOUR WAY OUT...
TAKE YOUR TIME...
blah
blah
THE PROP CASES ARE ALL THE SAME.
THEY'RE HE-ERE!!
vrrm vrrrrrm
I'M LEAVING. THEY CAN'T BE WORTH THE WAIT...
HOW LONG TILL WE GET OUR PROP CASES?
HURRY UP! HAND 'EM OUT ALREADY!
WHAT DO WE DO NOW, MISS WHITE?! THEY'RE STILL NOT HERE!
WE CAN'T KEEP THEM WAITING MUCH LONGER!

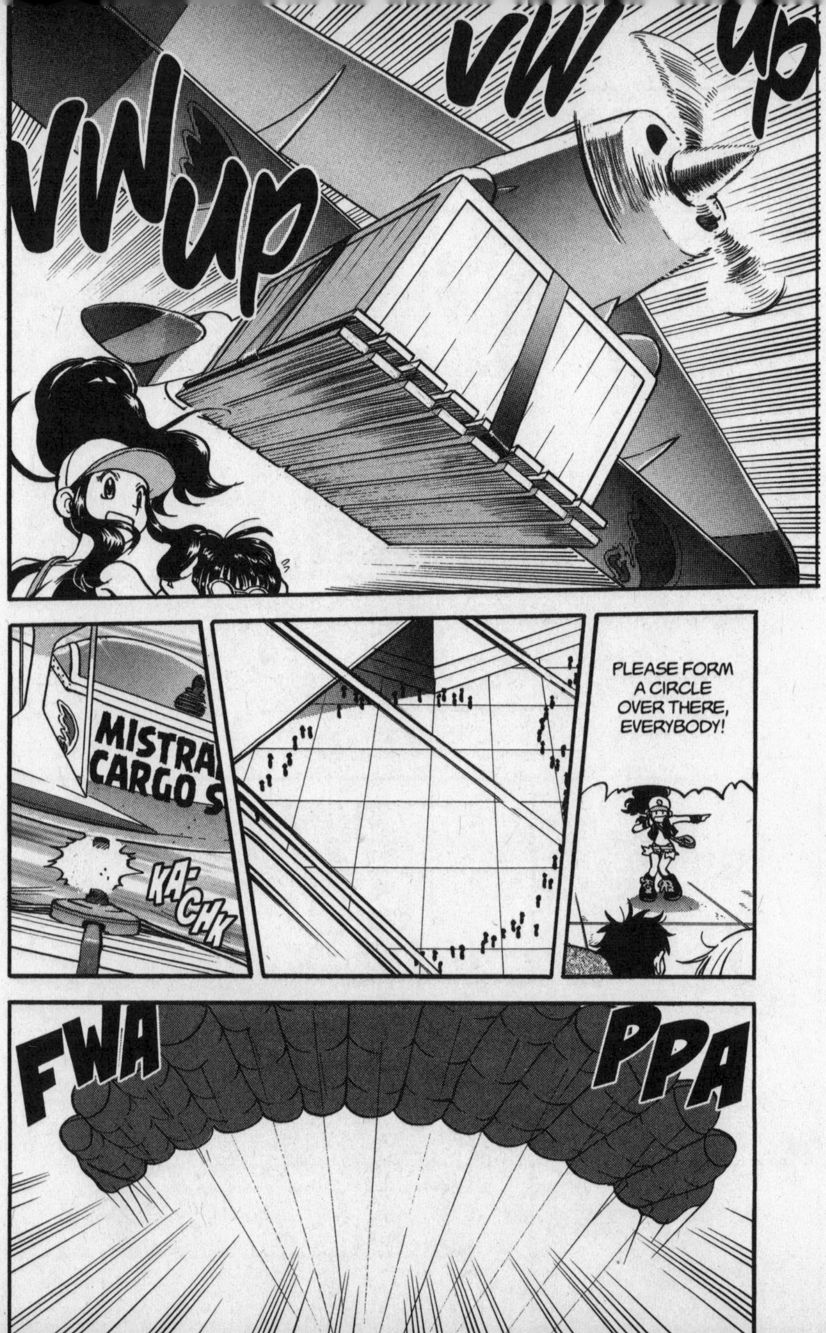
VWUP
VW
UP
MISTRA
CARGO S
KA-CHK
PLEASE FORM A CIRCLE OVER THERE, EVERYBODY!
FWA
PPA

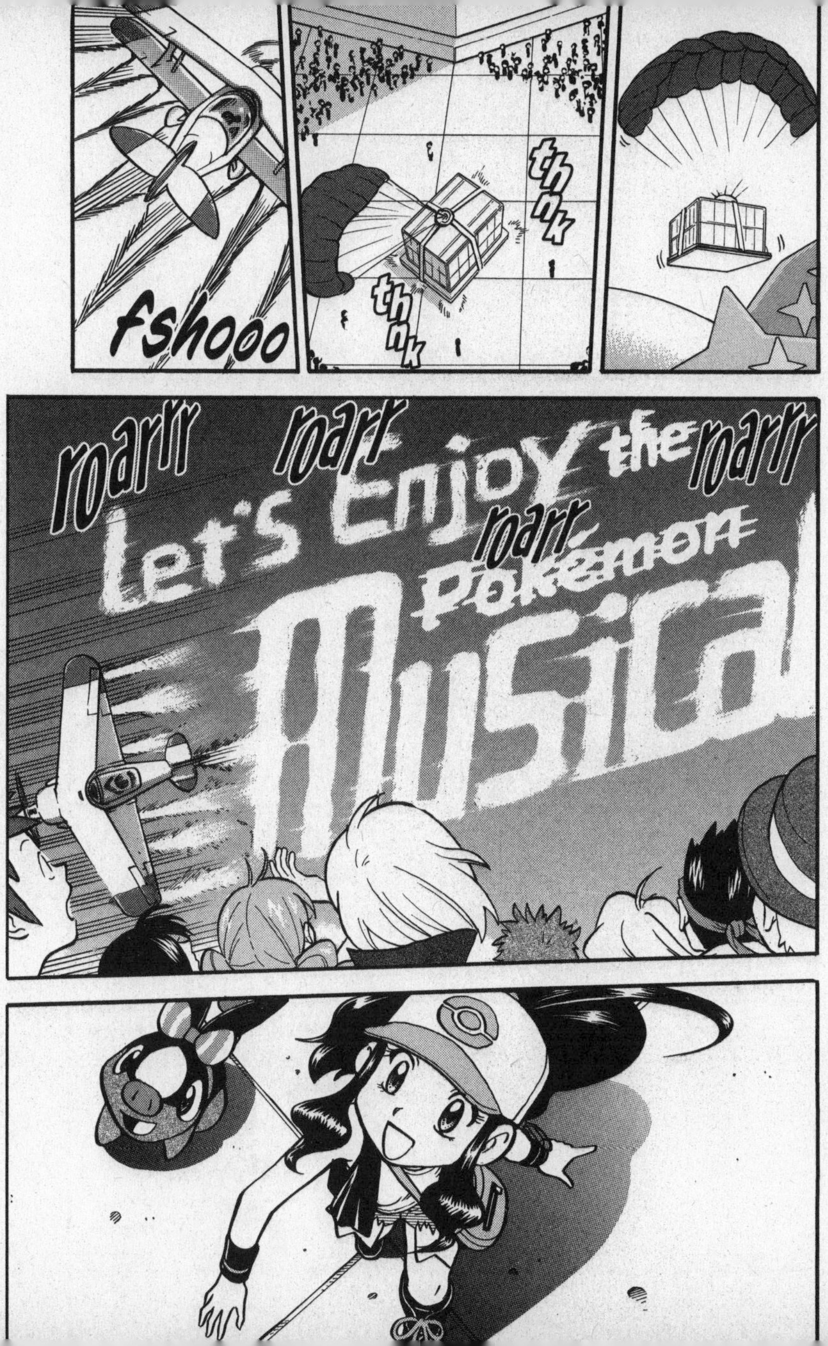
fshooo
thnk
thnk
roarrr
roarr
Let's Enjoy the Pokémon Musical
roarrr
roarr

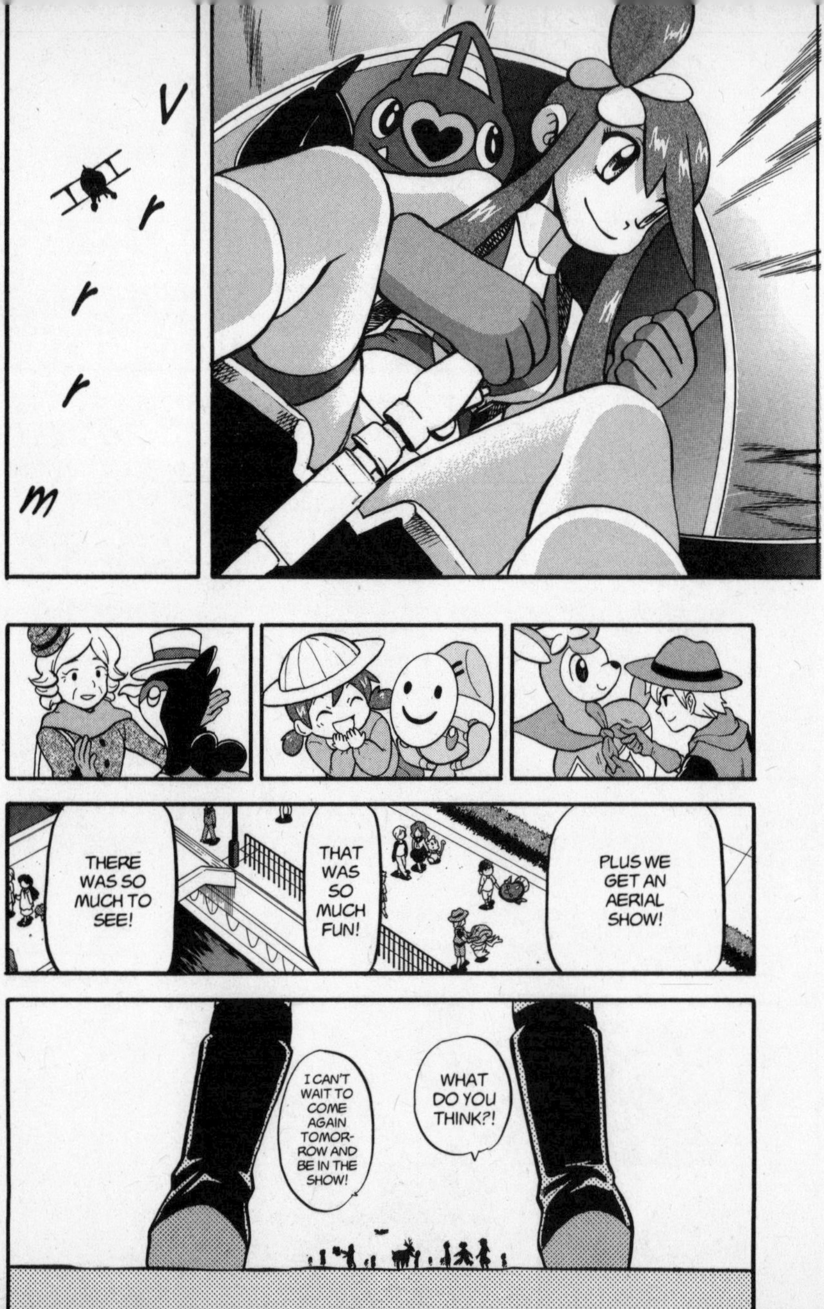

VRRRRM
THERE WAS SO MUCH TO SEE!
THAT WAS SO MUCH FUN!
PLUS WE GET AN AERIAL SHOW!
WHAT DO YOU THINK?!
I CAN'T WAIT TO COME AGAIN TOMOR-ROW AND BE IN THE SHOW!

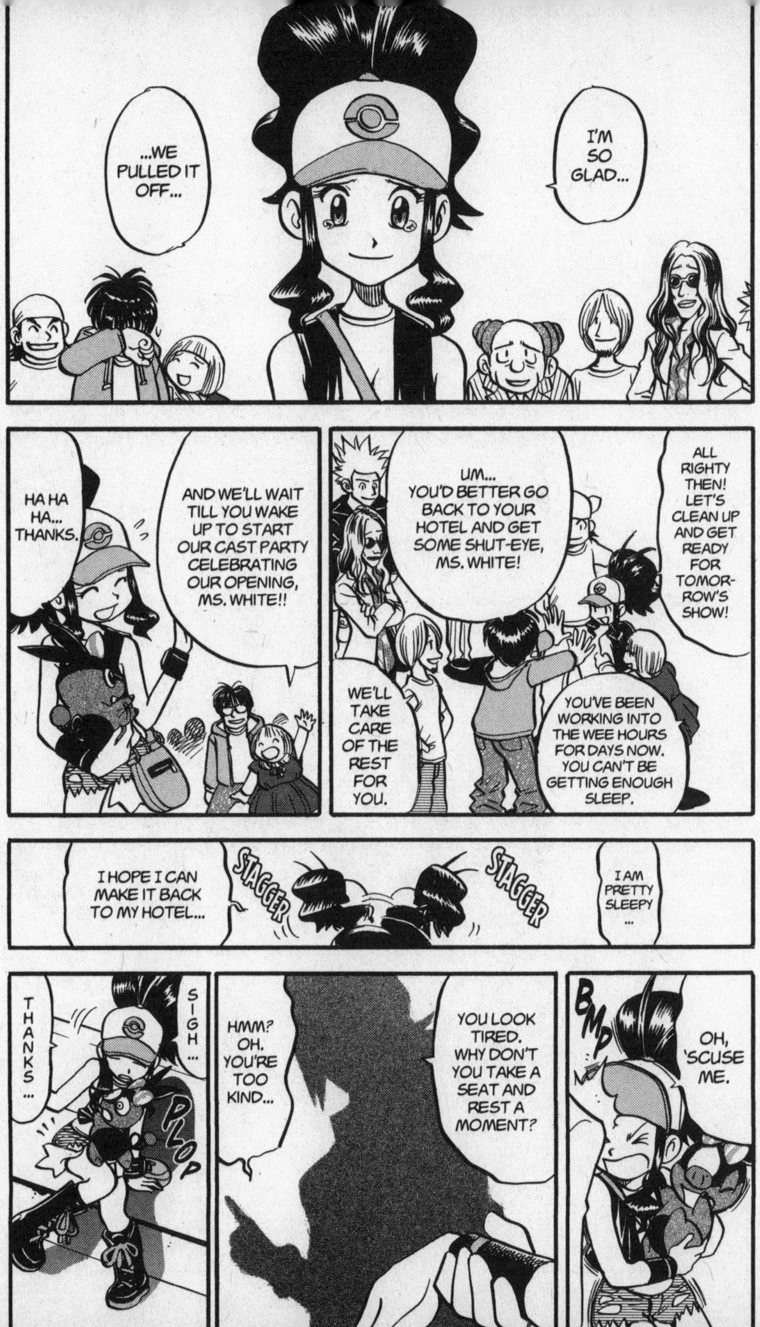
...WE PULLED IT OFF...
I'M SO GLAD...
HA HA HA... THANKS.
AND WE'LL WAIT TILL YOU WAKE UP TO START OUR CAST PARTY CELEBRATING OUR OPENING, MS. WHITE!!
UM... YOU'D BETTER GO BACK TO YOUR HOTEL AND GET SOME SHUT-EYE, MS. WHITE!
ALL RIGHTY THEN! LET'S CLEAN UP AND GET READY FOR TOMORROW'S SHOW!
WE'LL TAKE CARE OF THE REST FOR YOU.
YOU'VE BEEN WORKING INTO THE WEE HOURS FOR DAYS NOW. YOU CAN'T BE GETTING ENOUGH SLEEP.
I HOPE I CAN MAKE IT BACK TO MY HOTEL...
STAGGER
STAGGER
I AM PRETTY SLEEPY ...
BMP
OH, 'SCUSE ME.
YOU LOOK TIRED. WHY DON'T YOU TAKE A SEAT AND REST A MOMENT?
HMM? OH. YOU'RE TOO KIND...
SIGH...
THANKS...
PLOP

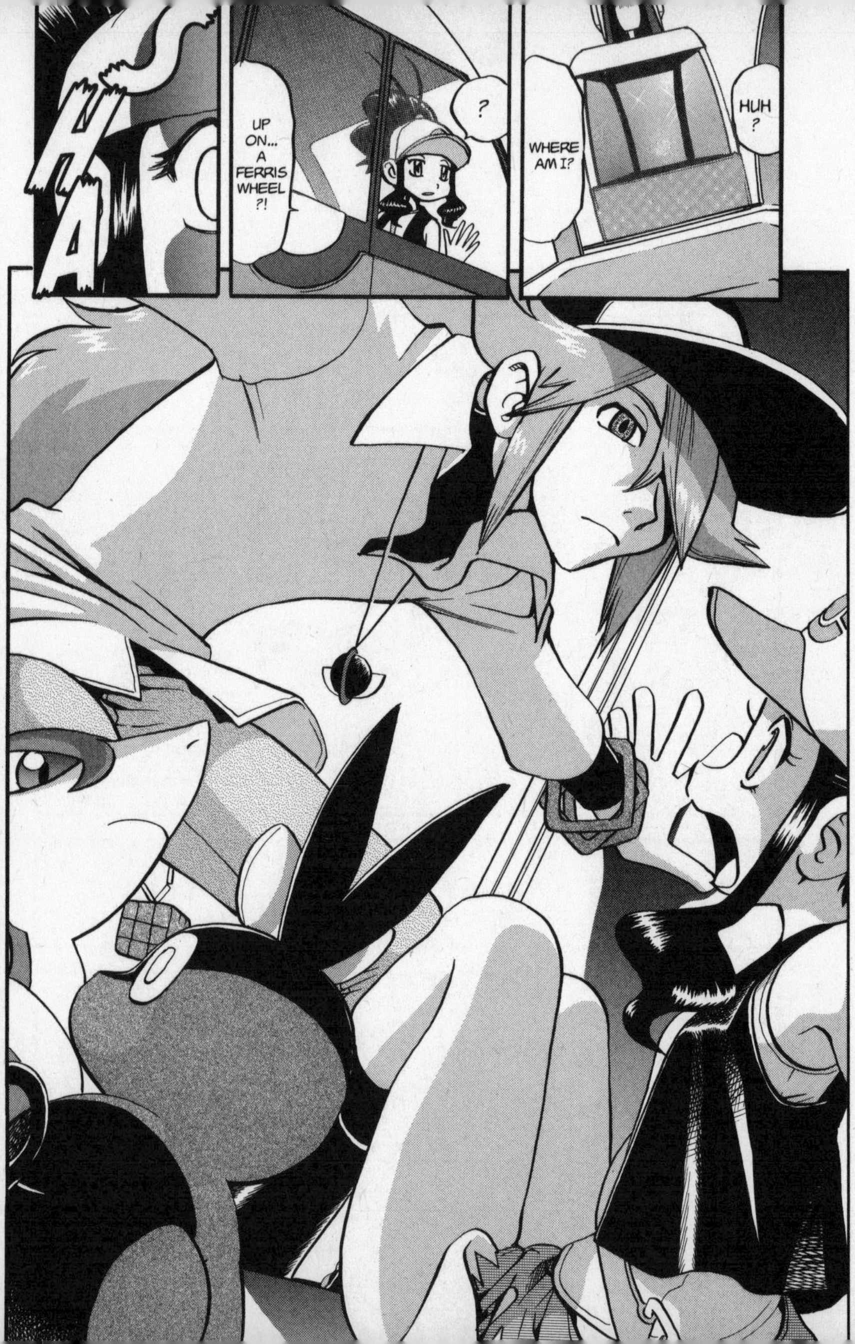
HUH?
WHERE AM I?
?
UP ON... A FERRIS WHEEL?!
HA

Adventure 24
Battle on a Roller Coaster

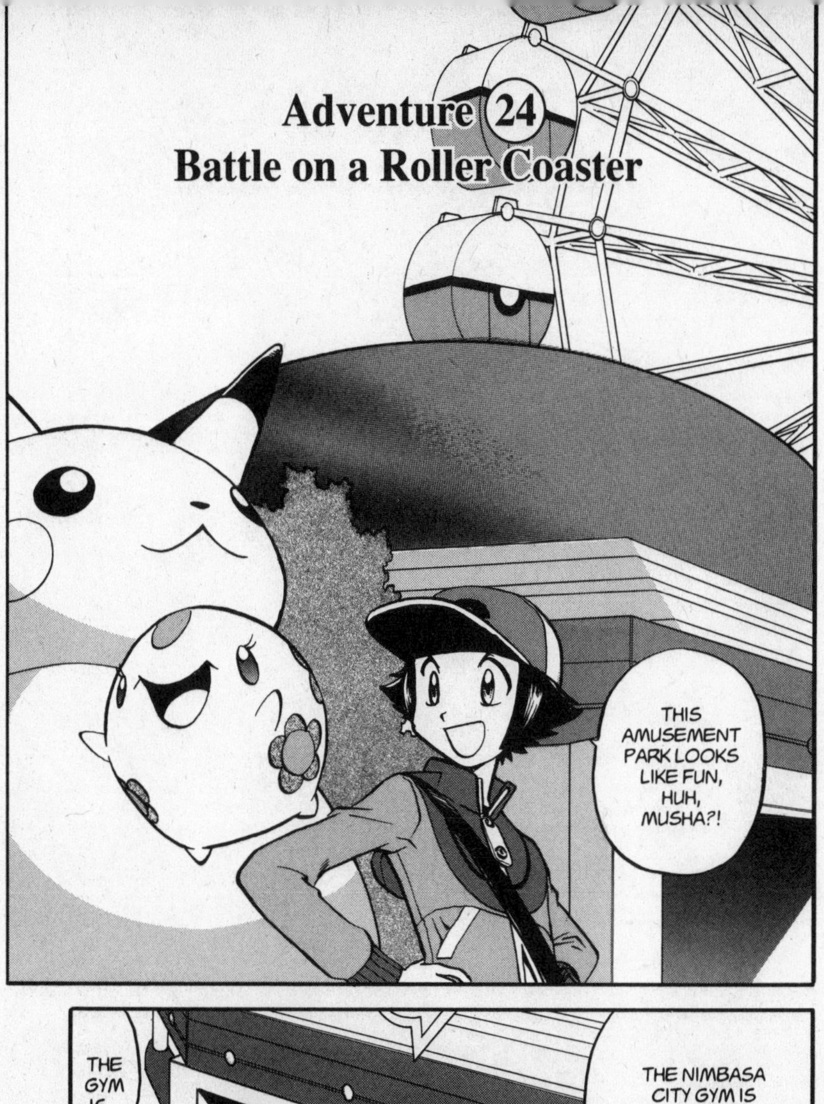
THIS AMUSEMENT PARK LOOKS LIKE FUN, HUH, MUSHA?!

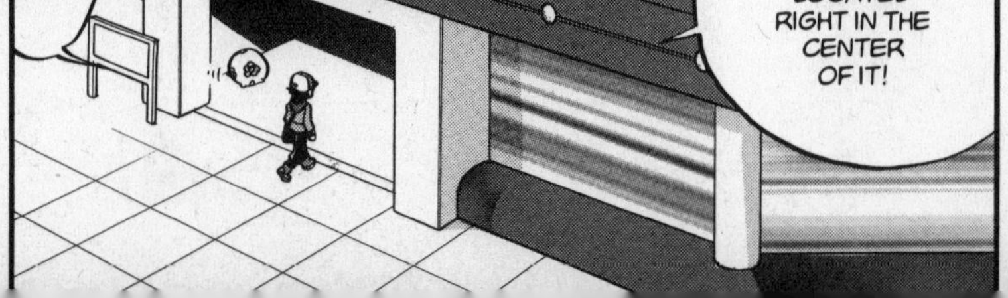
THE GYM IS...
THE NIMBASA CITY GYM IS LOCATED RIGHT IN THE CENTER OF IT!

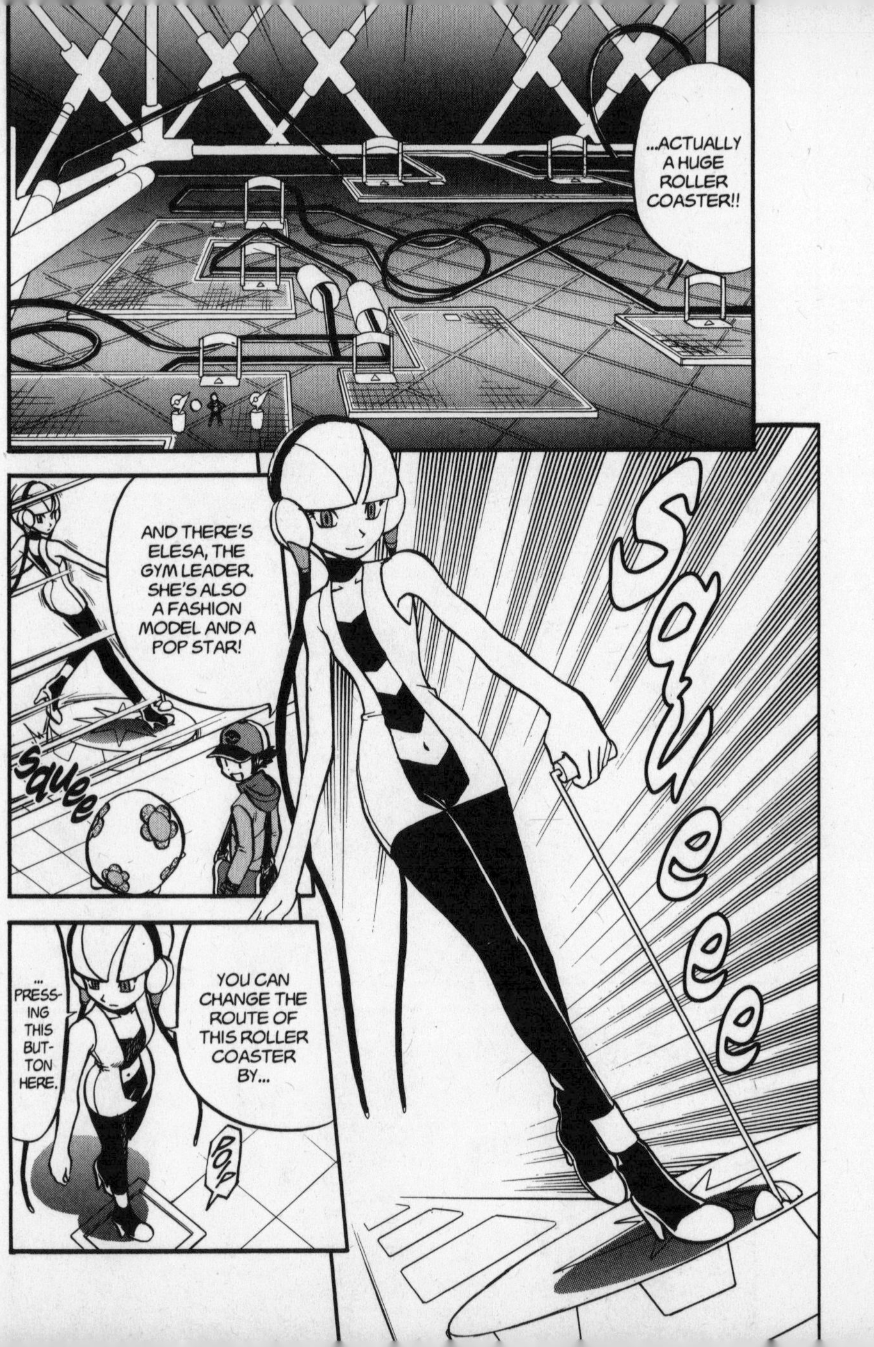
...ACTUALLY A HUGE ROLLER COASTER!!
AND THERE'S ELESA, THE GYM LEADER. SHE'S ALSO A FASHION MODEL AND A POP STAR!
squee
Squeeee
YOU CAN CHANGE THE ROUTE OF THIS ROLLER COASTER BY...
...PRESSING THIS BUTTON HERE.
POP

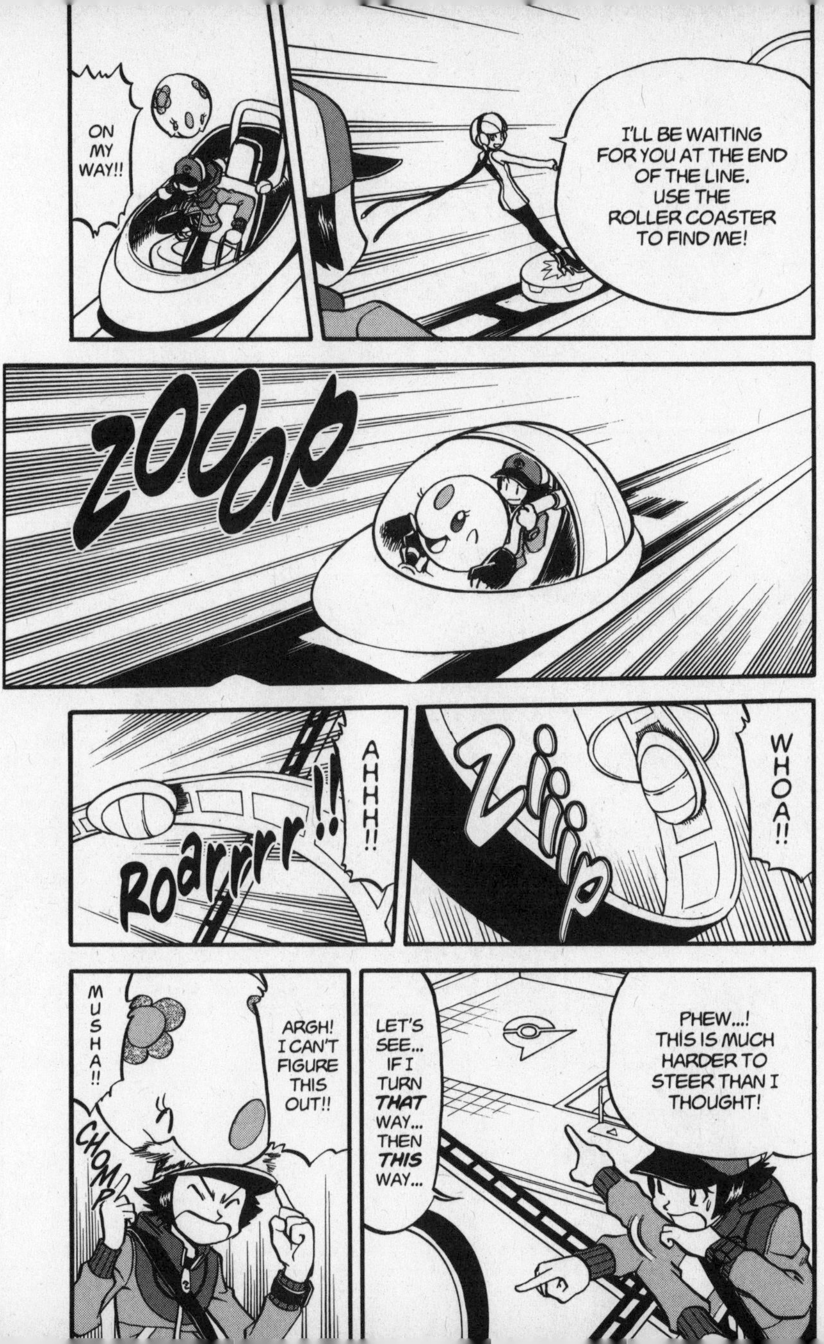
I'LL BE WAITING FOR YOU AT THE END OF THE LINE. USE THE ROLLER COASTER TO FIND ME!
ON MY WAY!!
ZOOOP
Roarrrr!!
AHHH!!
Ziiiip
WHOA!!
PHEW...! THIS IS MUCH HARDER TO STEER THAN I THOUGHT!
LET'S SEE... IF I TURN THAT WAY... THEN THIS WAY...
ARGH! I CAN'T FIGURE THIS OUT!!
MUSHA!!
CHOMP

SKREECH!

HUH
?

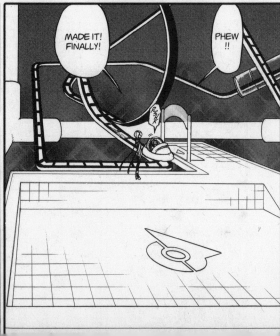

MADE IT!
FINALLY!

PHEW
!!

YOU
CAN'T
?

ELESA,
I CAN'T
UNLOCK
THE
SAFETY
HARNESS
!!

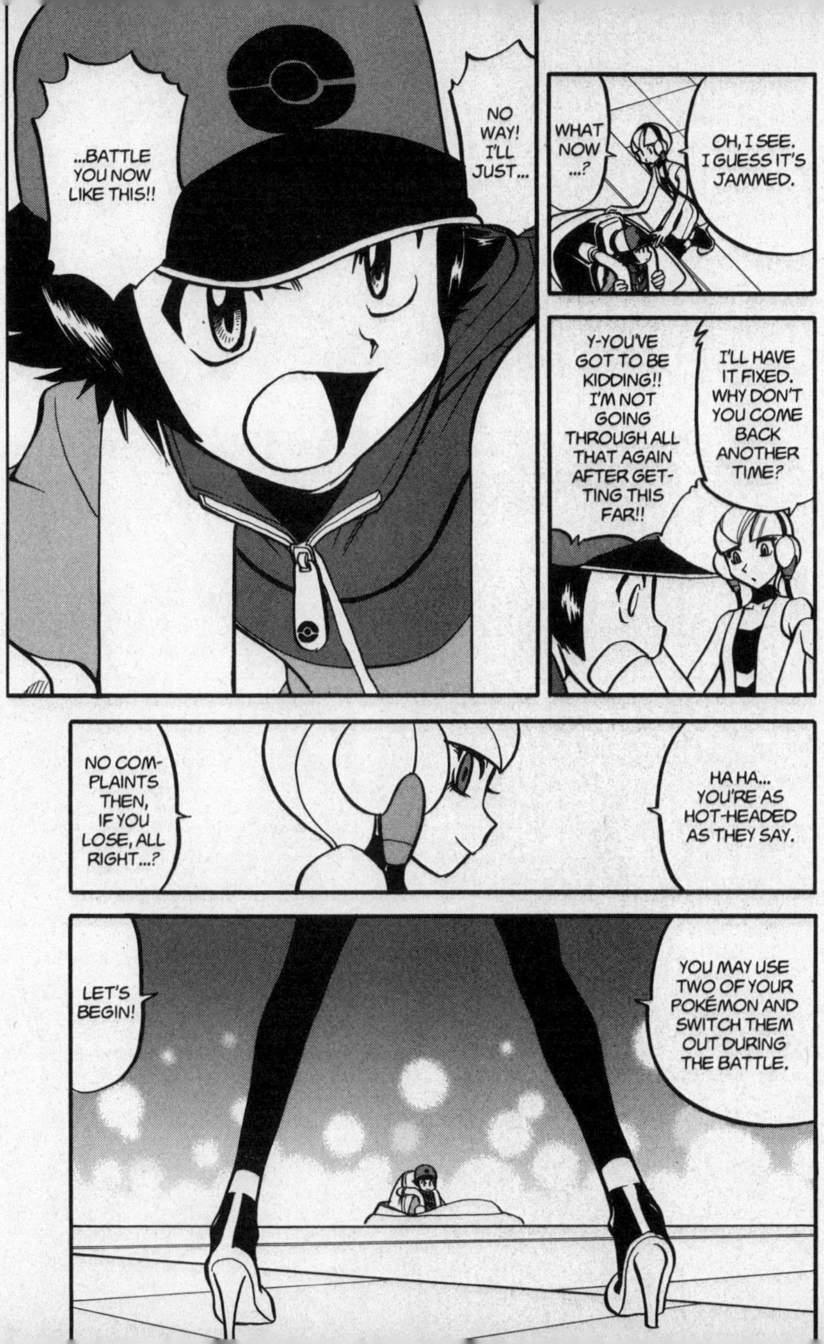
OH, I SEE. I GUESS IT'S JAMMED.
WHAT NOW ...?
I'LL HAVE IT FIXED. WHY DON'T YOU COME BACK ANOTHER TIME?
Y-YOU'VE GOT TO BE KIDDING!! I'M NOT GOING THROUGH ALL THAT AGAIN AFTER GETTING THIS FAR!!
NO WAY! I'LL JUST...
...BATTLE YOU NOW LIKE THIS!!
HA HA... YOU'RE AS HOT-HEADED AS THEY SAY.
NO COMPLAINTS THEN, IF YOU LOSE, ALL RIGHT...?
YOU MAY USE TWO OF YOUR POKÉMON AND SWITCH THEM OUT DURING THE BATTLE.
LET'S BEGIN!

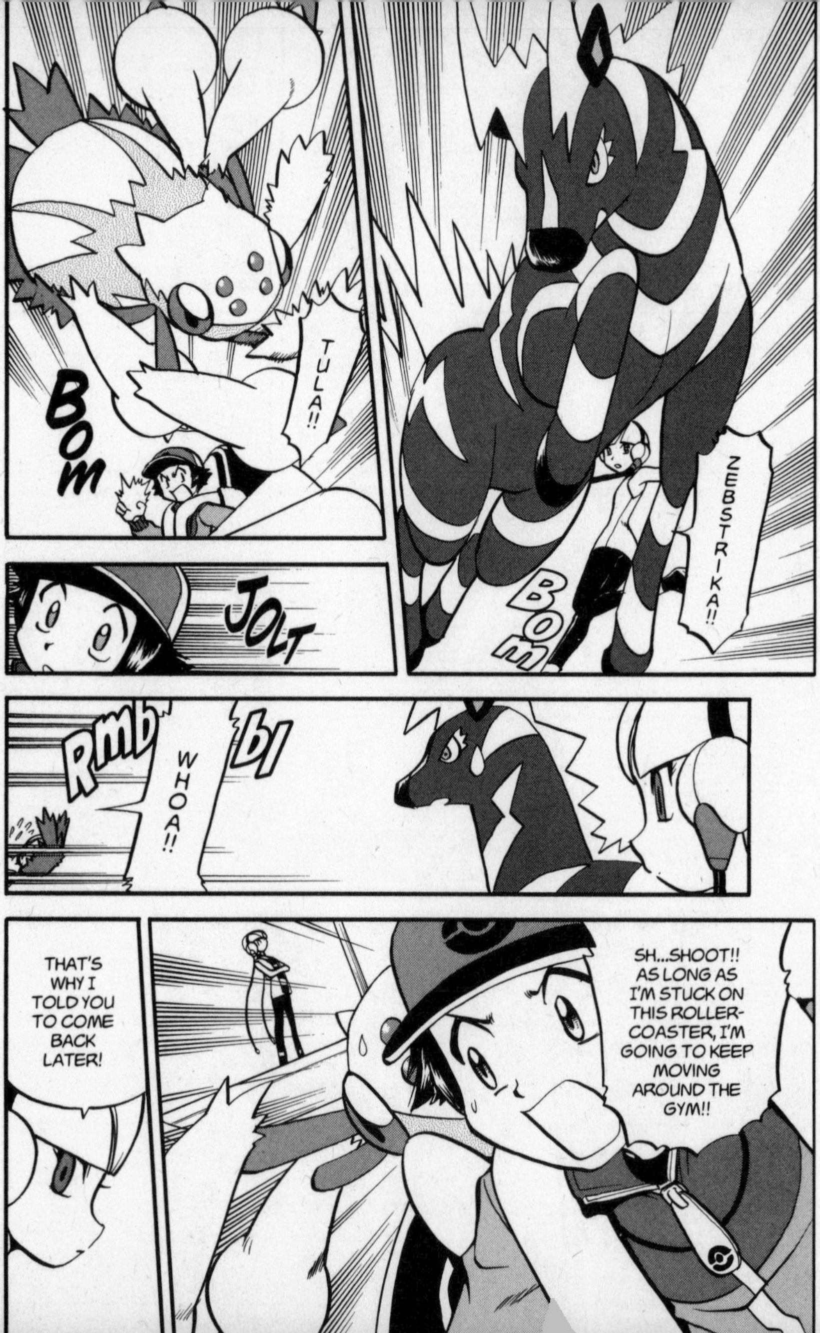
ZEBSTRIKA!!
BOM
TULA!!
BOM
JOLT
Rmb
bl
WHOA!!
SH...SHOOT!! AS LONG AS I'M STUCK ON THIS ROLLER-COASTER, I'M GOING TO KEEP MOVING AROUND THE GYM!!
THAT'S WHY I TOLD YOU TO COME BACK LATER!

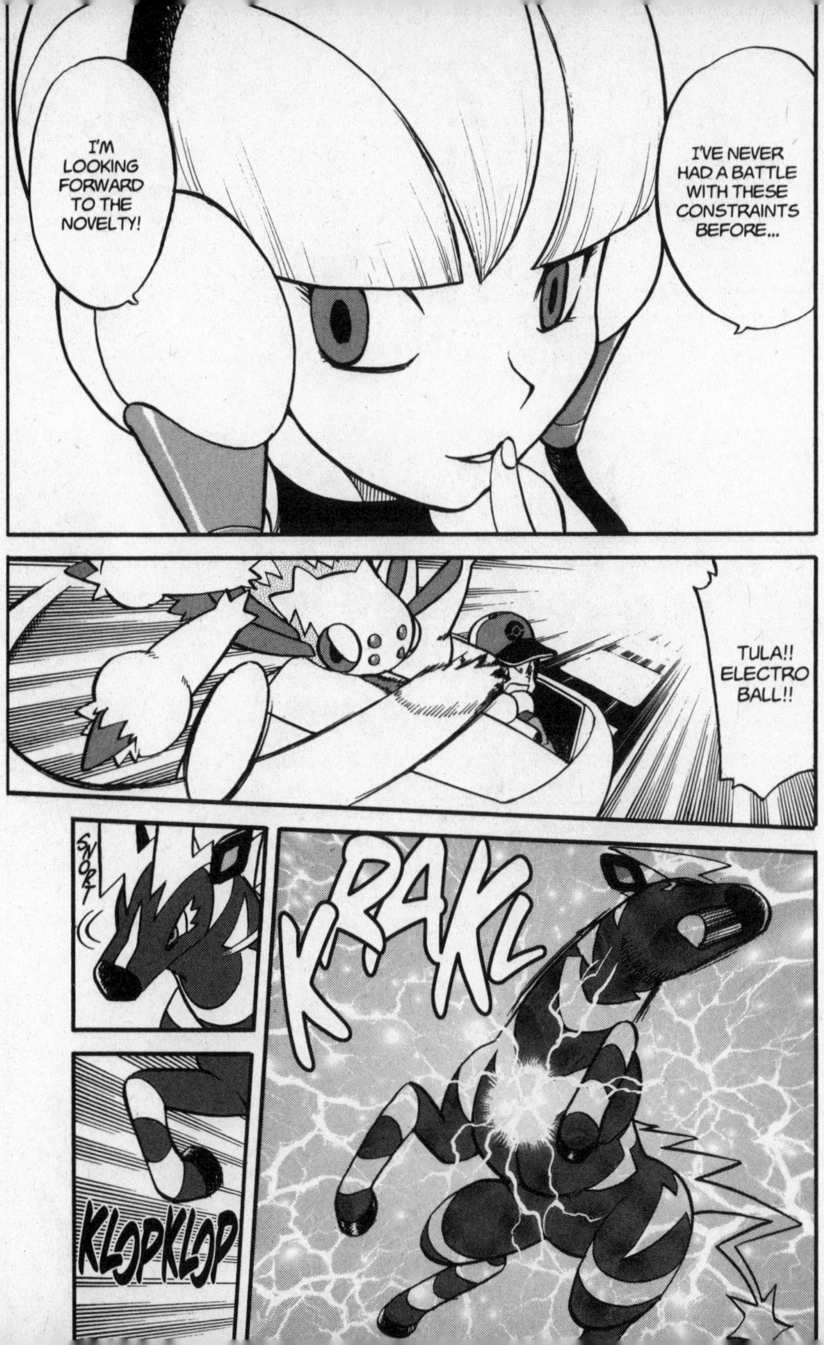
I'VE NEVER HAD A BATTLE WITH THESE CONSTRAINTS BEFORE...
I'M LOOKING FORWARD TO THE NOVELTY!
TULA!! ELECTRO BALL!!
SNORT
KRAKL
KLOPKLOP

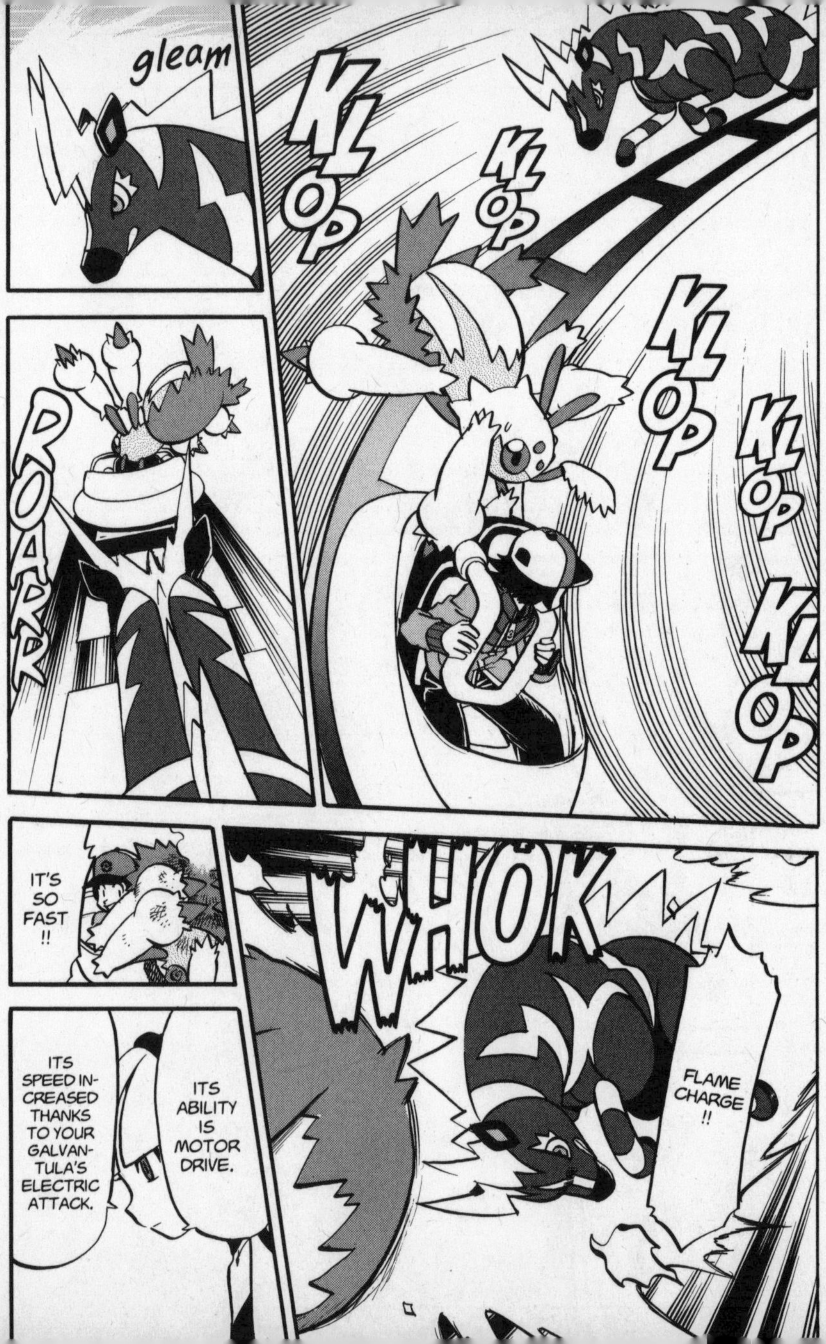
gleam
KLOP
KLOP
KLOP
KLOP
KLOP
KLOP
ROARR
IT'S SO FAST !!
WHOK
FLAME CHARGE !!
ITS ABILITY IS MOTOR DRIVE.
ITS SPEED IN-CREASED THANKS TO YOUR GALVAN-TULA'S ELECTRIC ATTACK.

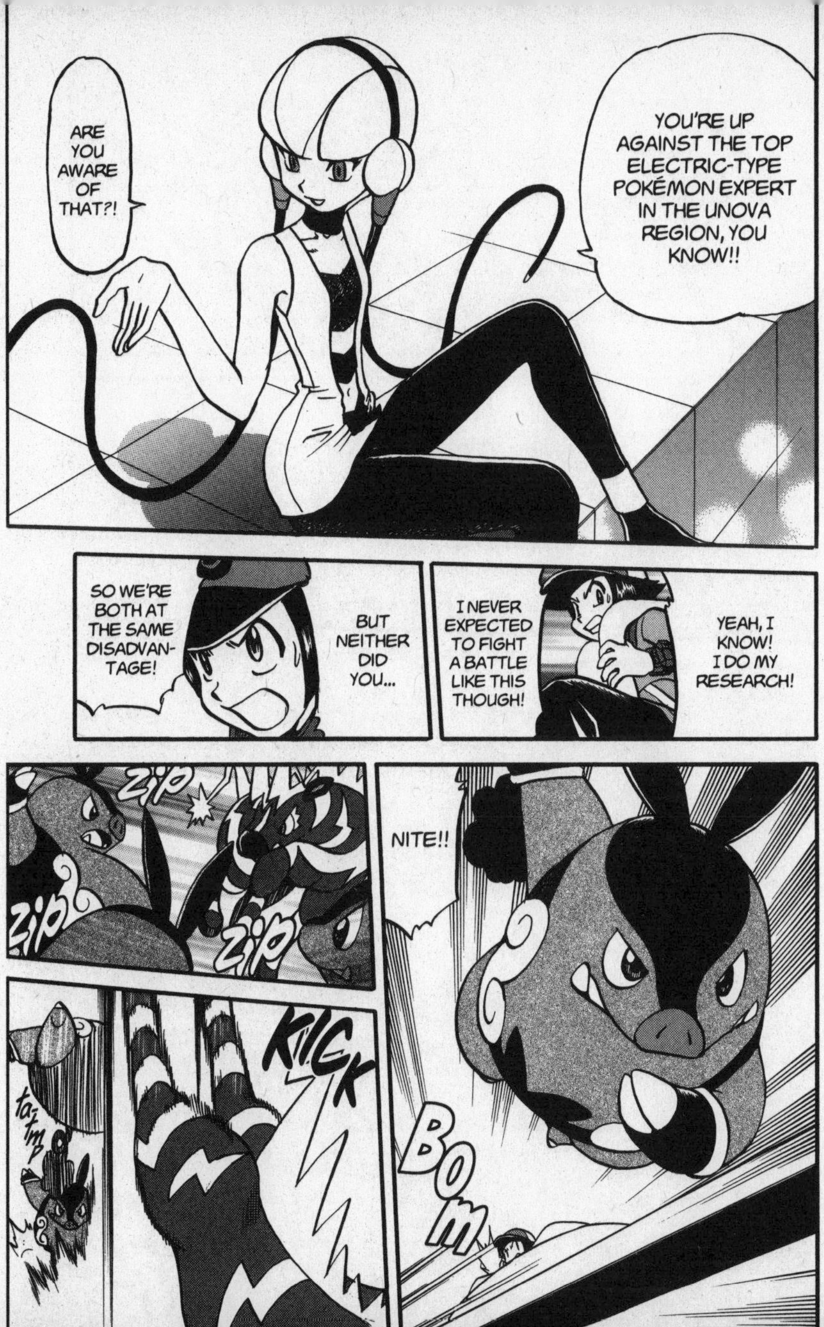
ARE YOU AWARE OF THAT?!
YOU'RE UP AGAINST THE TOP ELECTRIC-TYPE POKÉMON EXPERT IN THE UNOVA REGION, YOU KNOW!!
SO WE'RE BOTH AT THE SAME DISADVANTAGE!
BUT NEITHER DID YOU...
I NEVER EXPECTED TO FIGHT A BATTLE LIKE THIS THOUGH!
YEAH, I KNOW! I DO MY RESEARCH!
ZIP
ZIP
ZIP
NITE!!
KICK
BOM

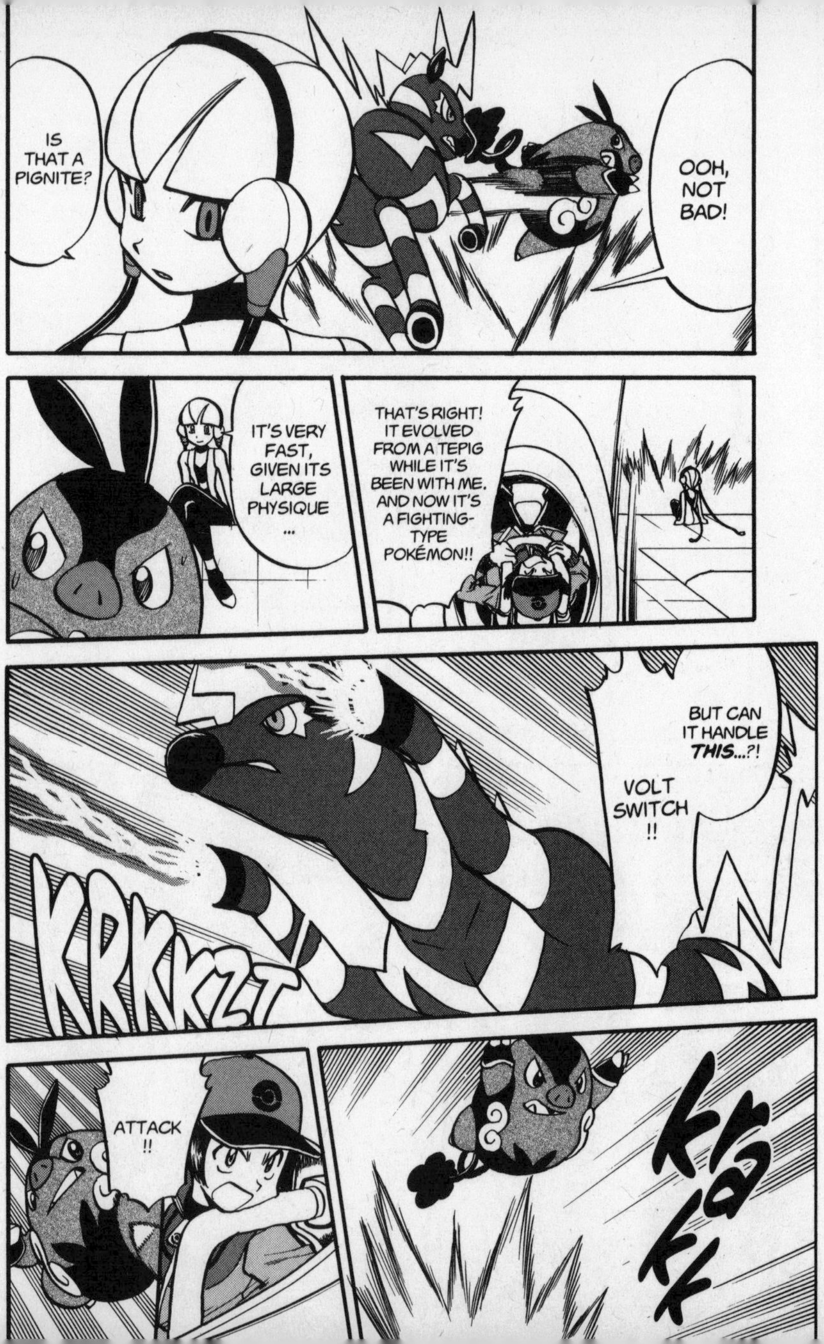

IS THAT A PIGNITE?
OOH, NOT BAD!
IT'S VERY FAST, GIVEN ITS LARGE PHYSIQUE ...
THAT'S RIGHT! IT EVOLVED FROM A TEPIG WHILE IT'S BEEN WITH ME. AND NOW IT'S A FIGHTING-TYPE POKÉMON!!
BUT CAN IT HANDLE ***THIS***...?!
VOLT SWITCH !!
KRKKZZT
ATTACK !!
KRAKK

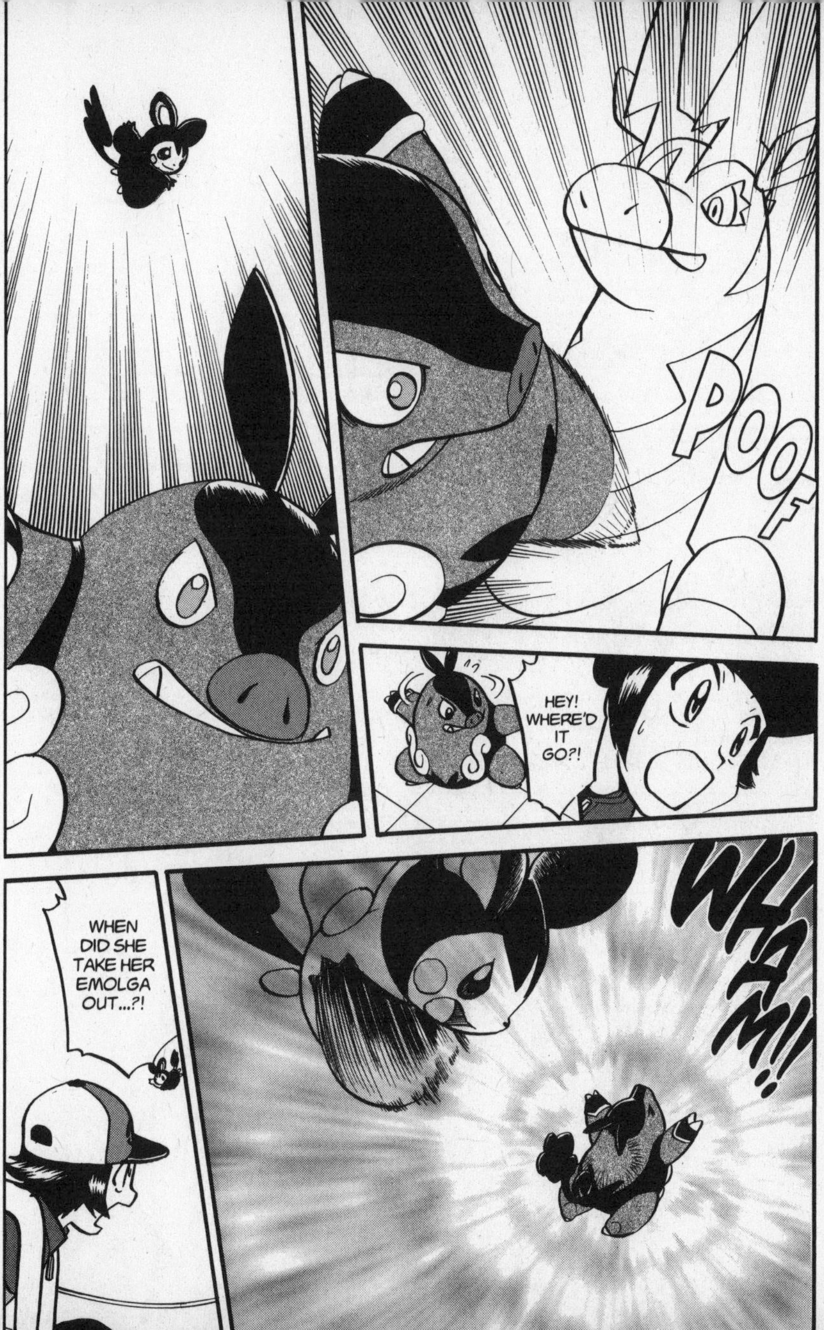

POOF
HEY! WHERE'D IT GO?!
WHAM!!
WHEN DID SHE TAKE HER EMOLGA OUT...?!

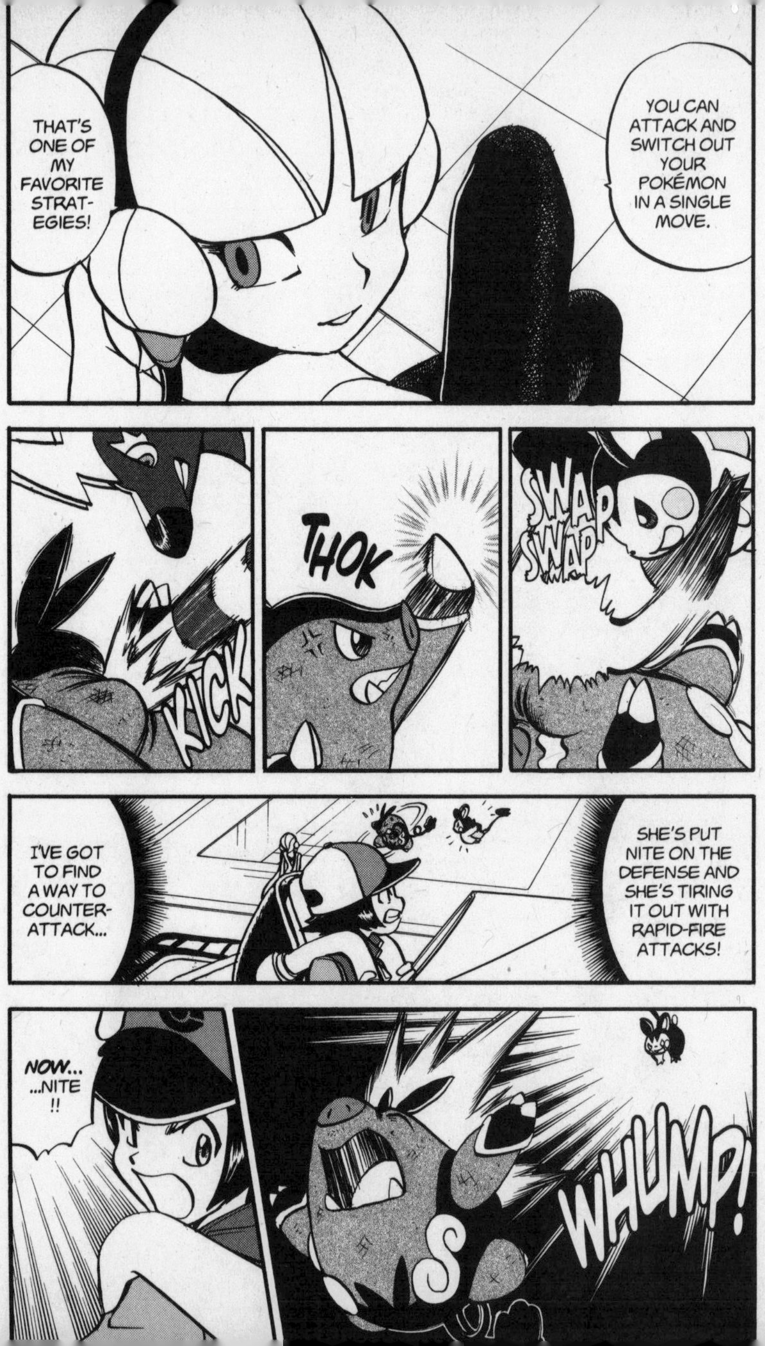
YOU CAN ATTACK AND SWITCH OUT YOUR POKÉMON IN A SINGLE MOVE.
THAT'S ONE OF MY FAVORITE STRAT-EGIES!
KICK
THOK
SWAP SWAP
SHE'S PUT NITE ON THE DEFENSE AND SHE'S TIRING IT OUT WITH RAPID-FIRE ATTACKS!
I'VE GOT TO FIND A WAY TO COUNTER-ATTACK...
WHUMP!
NOW... ...NITE !!

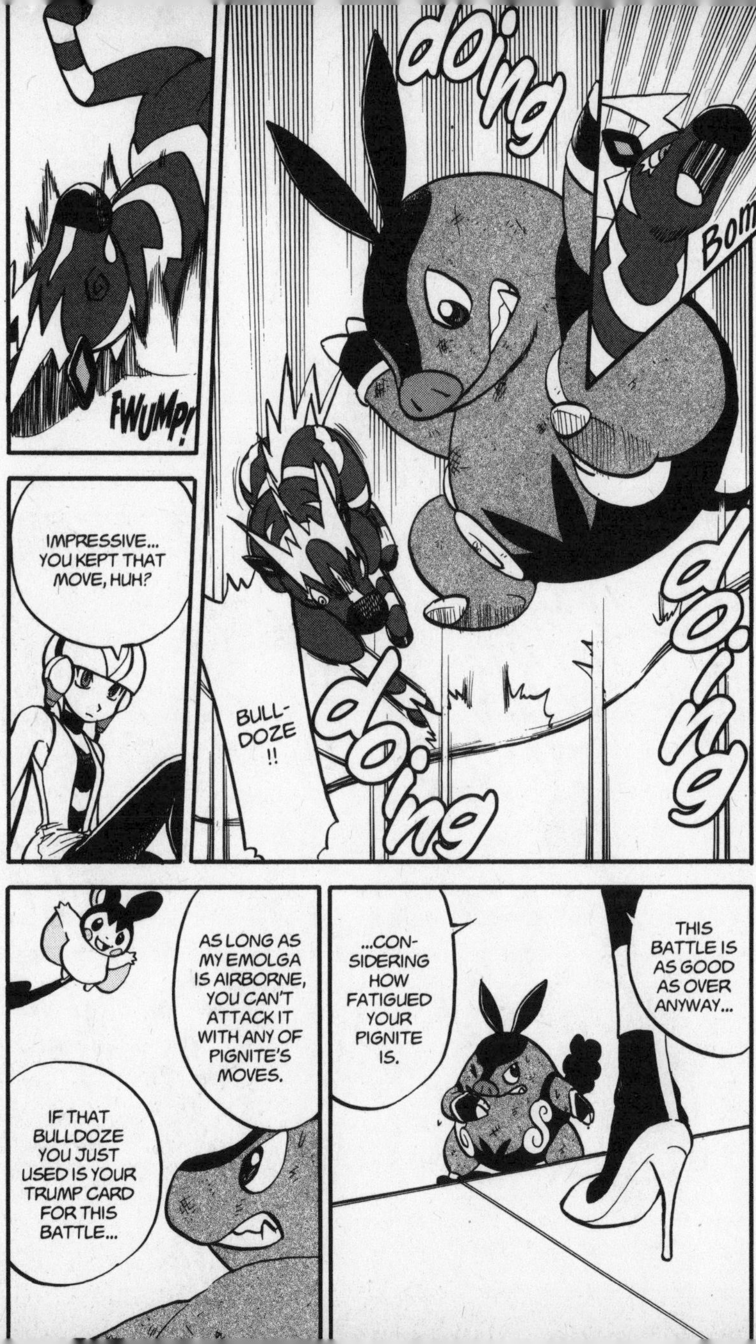
FWUMP!
doing
Bom
IMPRESSIVE... YOU KEPT THAT MOVE, HUH?
BULL-DOZE !!
doing
doing
AS LONG AS MY EMOLGA IS AIRBORNE, YOU CAN'T ATTACK IT WITH ANY OF PIGNITE'S MOVES.
IF THAT BULLDOZE YOU JUST USED IS YOUR TRUMP CARD FOR THIS BATTLE...
...CON-SIDERING HOW FATIGUED YOUR PIGNITE IS.
THIS BATTLE IS AS GOOD AS OVER ANYWAY...

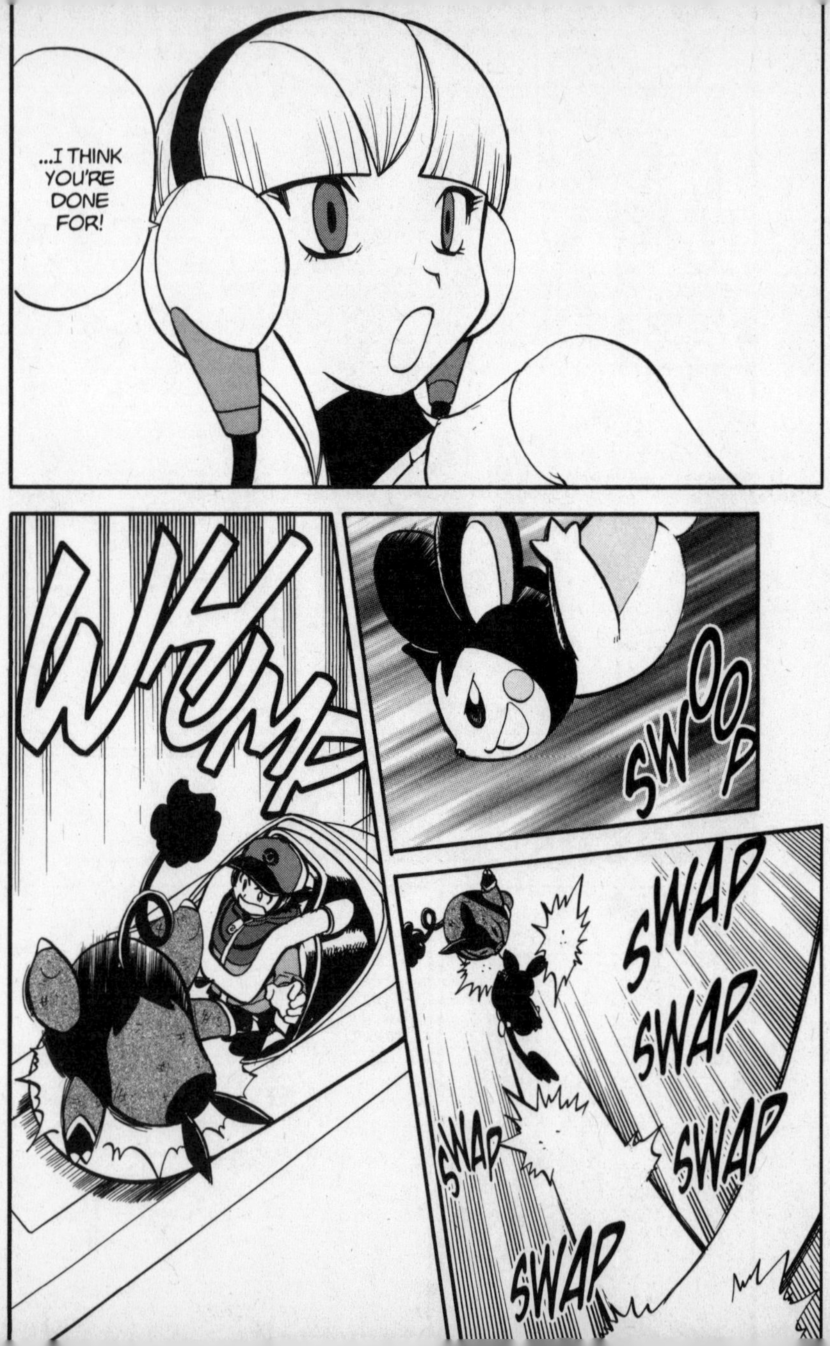
...I THINK YOU'RE DONE FOR!
WUMP
SWOOP
SWAP
SWAP
SWAP
SWAP
SWAP
SWAP

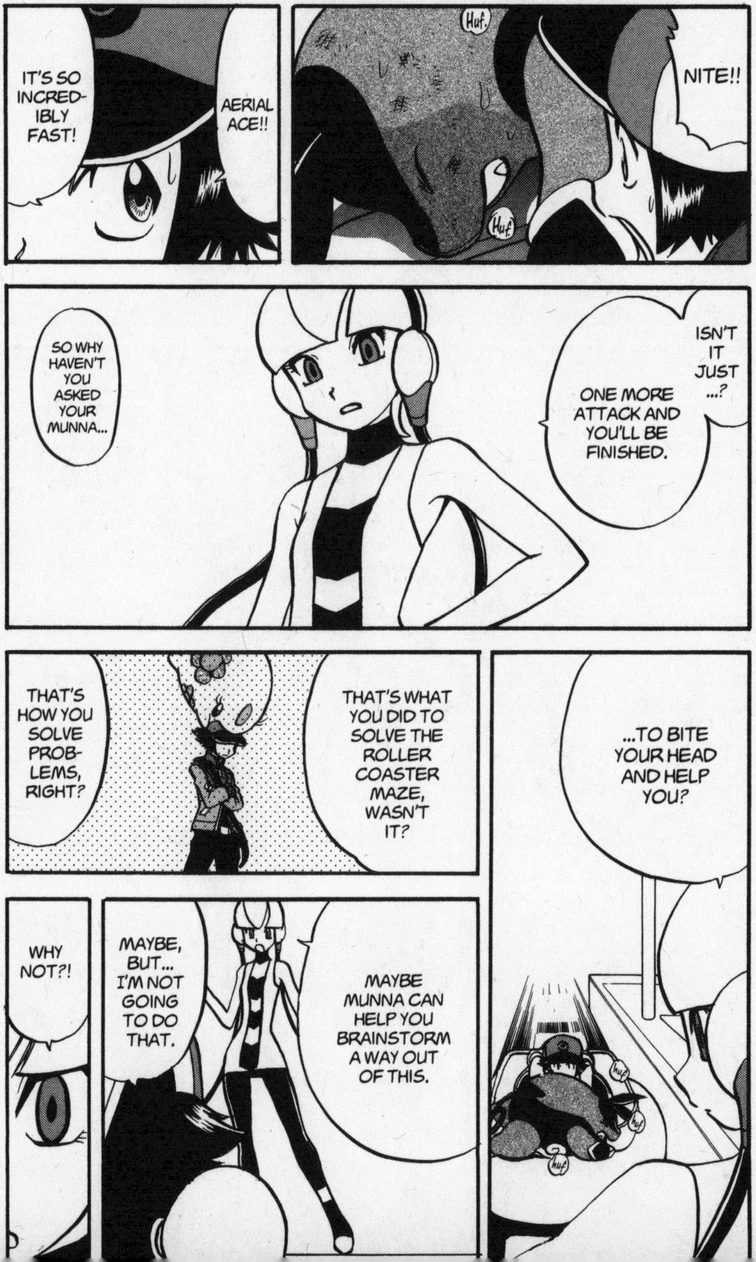
Huf.
Huf.
NITE!!
AERIAL ACE!!
IT'S SO INCREDIBLY FAST!
ISN'T IT JUST ...?
ONE MORE ATTACK AND YOU'LL BE FINISHED.
SO WHY HAVEN'T YOU ASKED YOUR MUNNA...
...TO BITE YOUR HEAD AND HELP YOU?
huf
huf
huf
THAT'S WHAT YOU DID TO SOLVE THE ROLLER COASTER MAZE, WASN'T IT?
THAT'S HOW YOU SOLVE PROB-LEMS, RIGHT?
MAYBE MUNNA CAN HELP YOU BRAINSTORM A WAY OUT OF THIS.
MAYBE, BUT... I'M NOT GOING TO DO THAT.
WHY NOT?!

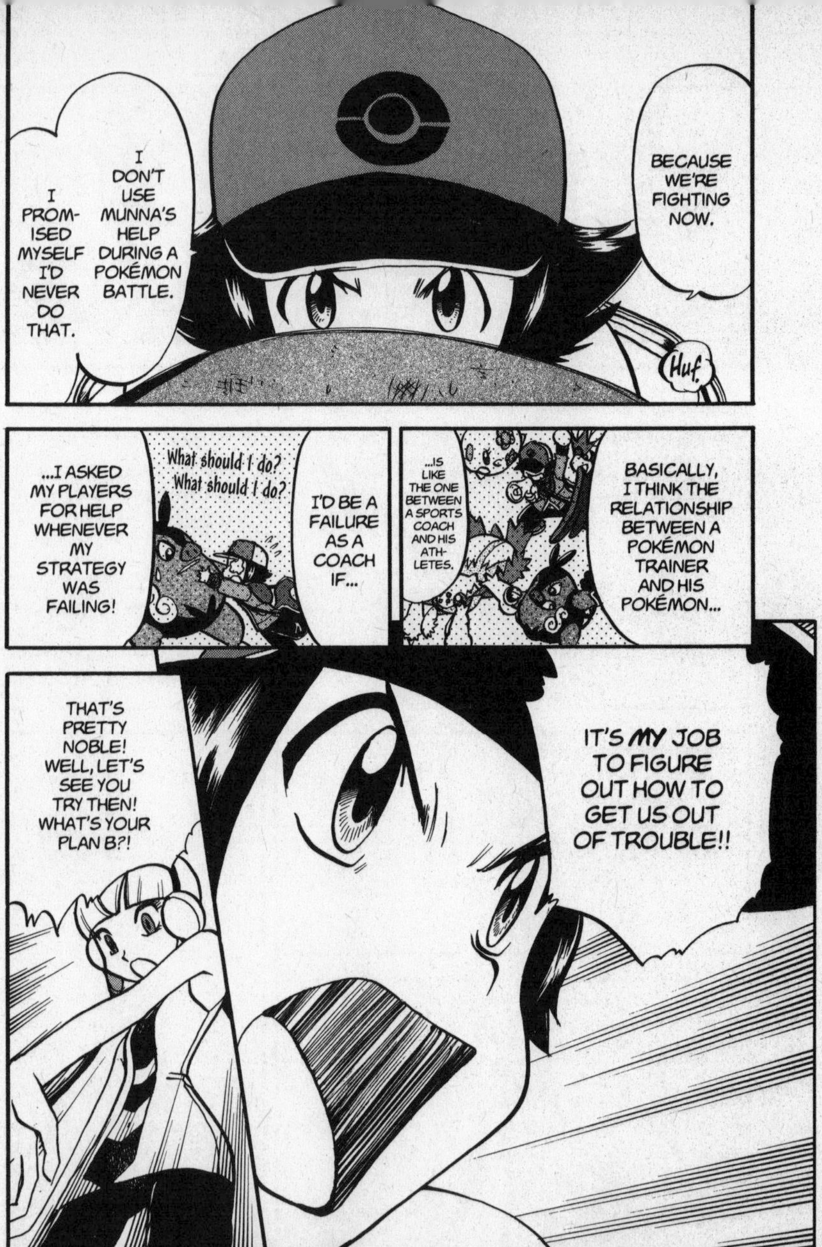

BECAUSE WE'RE FIGHTING NOW.
Huf.
I DON'T USE MUNNA'S HELP DURING A POKÉMON BATTLE.
I PROMISED MYSELF I'D NEVER DO THAT.
BASICALLY, I THINK THE RELATIONSHIP BETWEEN A POKÉMON TRAINER AND HIS POKÉMON...
...IS LIKE THE ONE BETWEEN A SPORTS COACH AND HIS ATHLETES.
I'D BE A FAILURE AS A COACH IF...
What should I do? What should I do?
...I ASKED MY PLAYERS FOR HELP WHENEVER MY STRATEGY WAS FAILING!
IT'S *MY* JOB TO FIGURE OUT HOW TO GET US OUT OF TROUBLE!!
THAT'S PRETTY NOBLE! WELL, LET'S SEE YOU TRY THEN! WHAT'S YOUR PLAN B?!

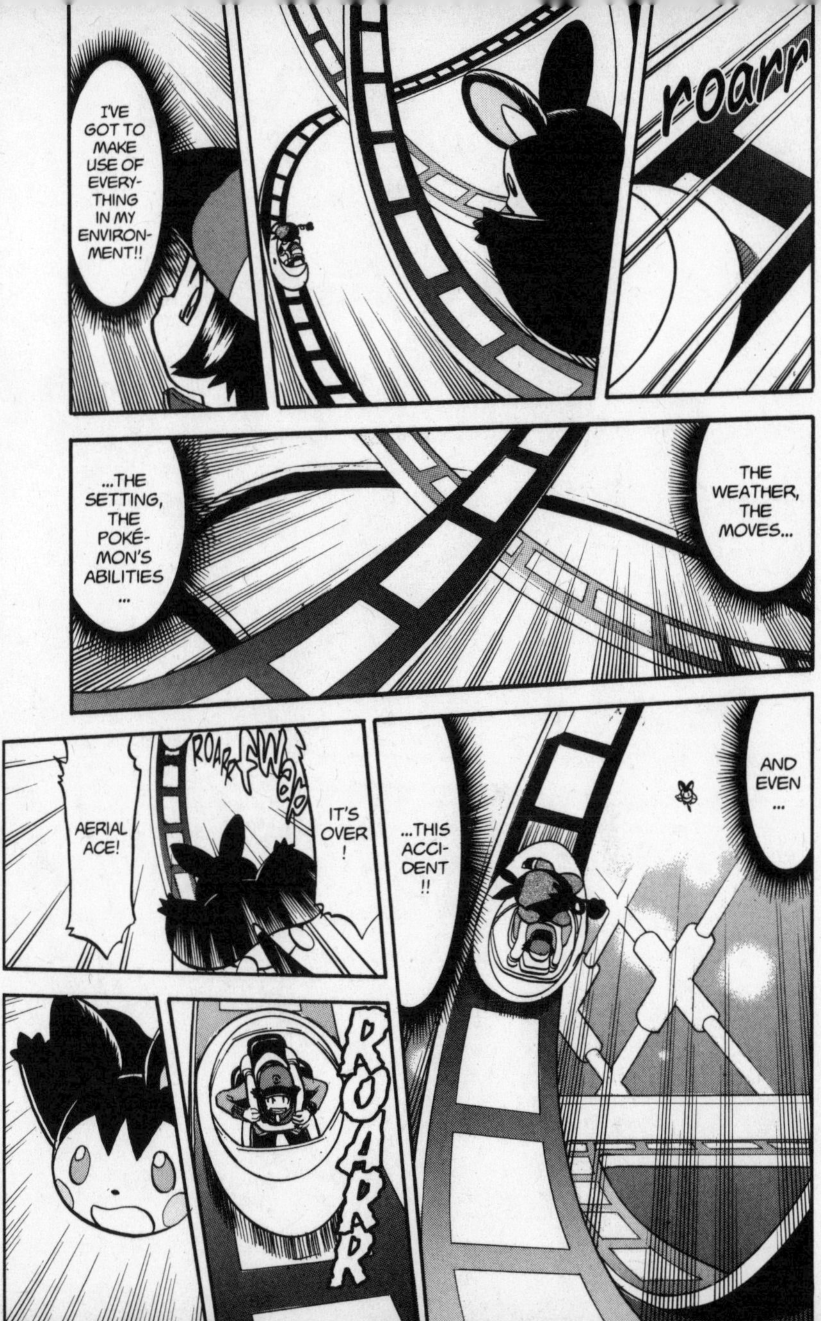
roarr
I'VE GOT TO MAKE USE OF EVERY-THING IN MY ENVIRON-MENT!!
THE WEATHER, THE MOVES...
...THE SETTING, THE POKÉ-MON'S ABILITIES ...
AND EVEN ...
...THIS ACCI-DENT !!
IT'S OVER !
ROARR
AERIAL ACE!
ROAARR

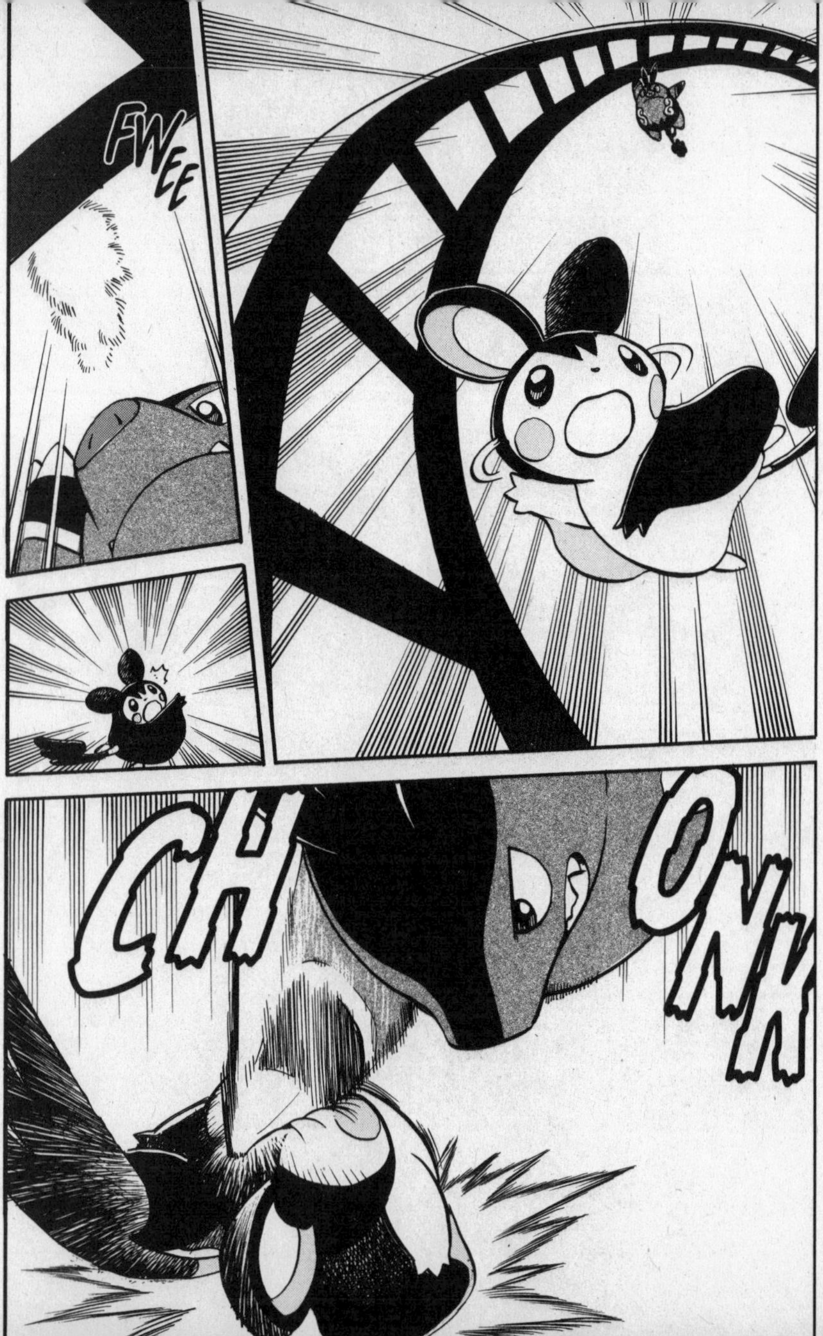
FWEE
CHONK

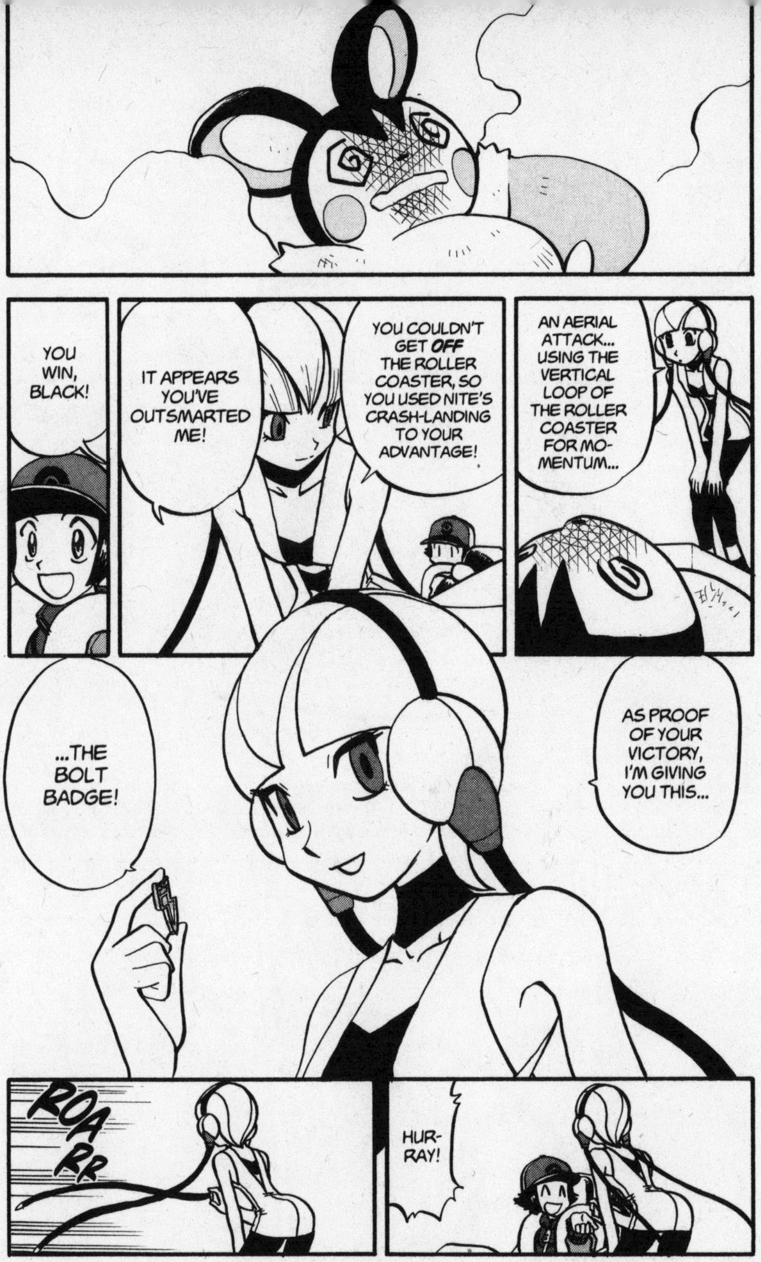
YOU WIN, BLACK!
IT APPEARS YOU'VE OUTSMARTED ME!
YOU COULDN'T GET OFF THE ROLLER COASTER, SO YOU USED NITE'S CRASH-LANDING TO YOUR ADVANTAGE!
AN AERIAL ATTACK... USING THE VERTICAL LOOP OF THE ROLLER COASTER FOR MO-MENTUM...
AS PROOF OF YOUR VICTORY, I'M GIVING YOU THIS...
...THE BOLT BADGE!
ROARRR
HUR-RAY!

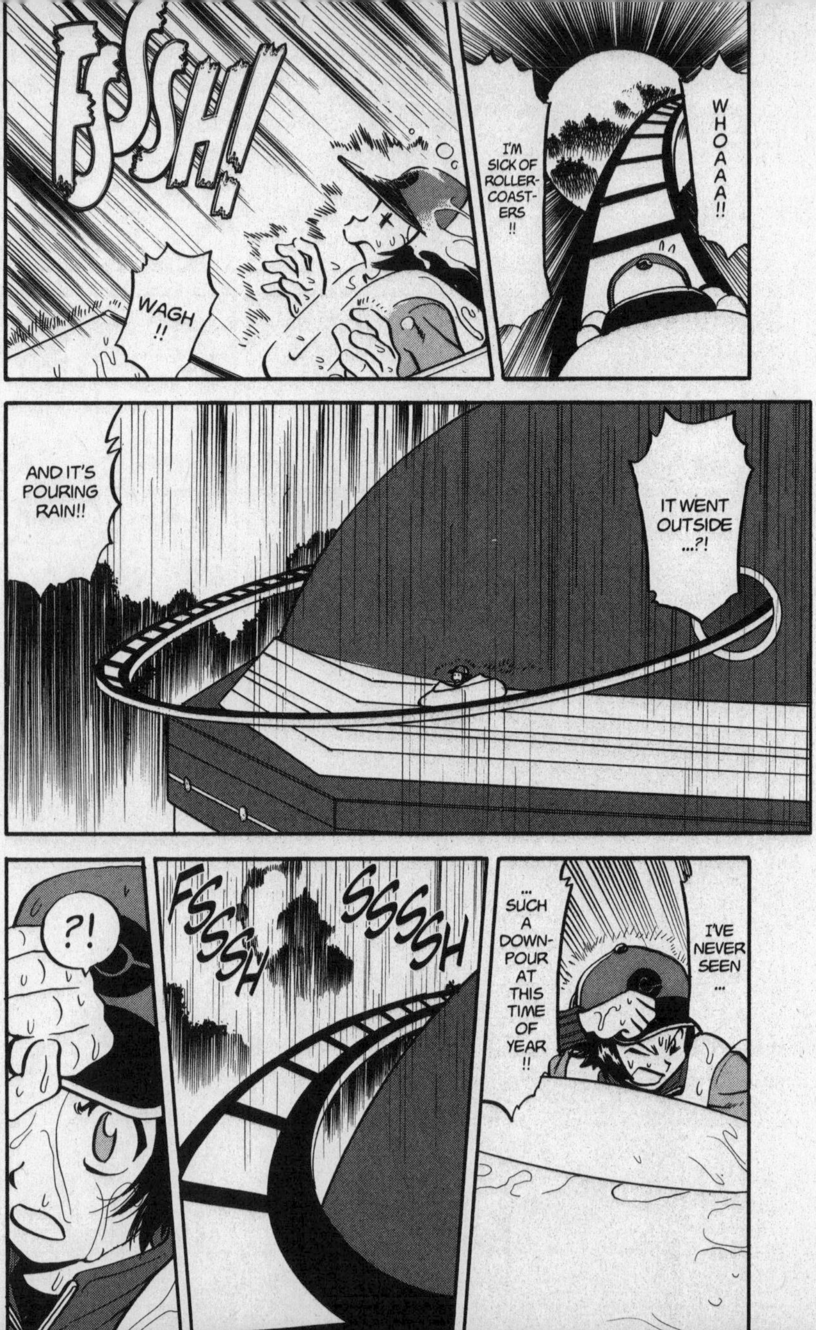
WHOAAAA!!
I'M SICK OF ROLLER-COASTERS!!
FSSH!
WAGH!!
IT WENT OUTSIDE...?!
AND IT'S POURING RAIN!!
I'VE NEVER SEEN...
...SUCH A DOWNPOUR AT THIS TIME OF YEAR!!
FSSSH
SSSSH
?!

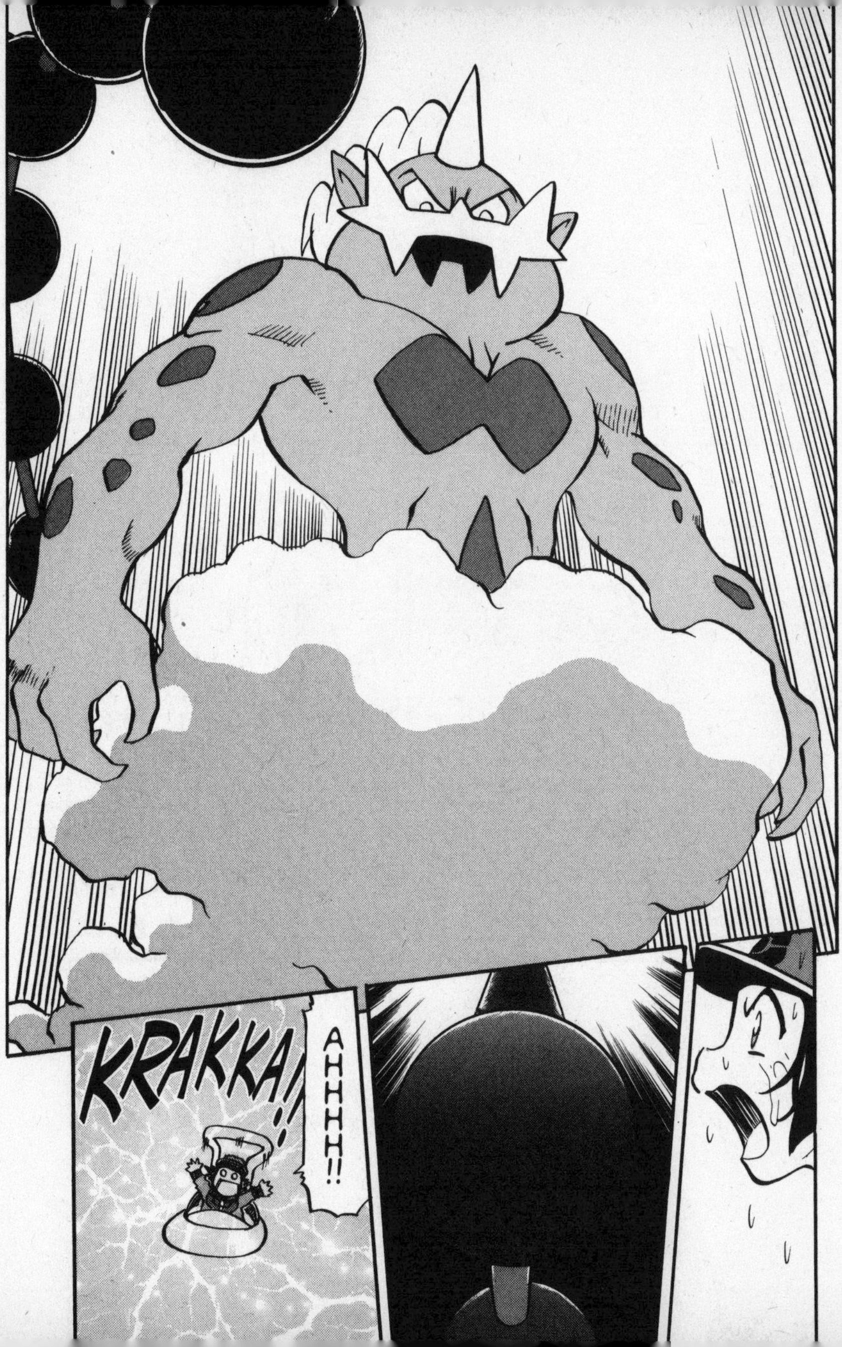
KRAKKA!!
AHHHH!!

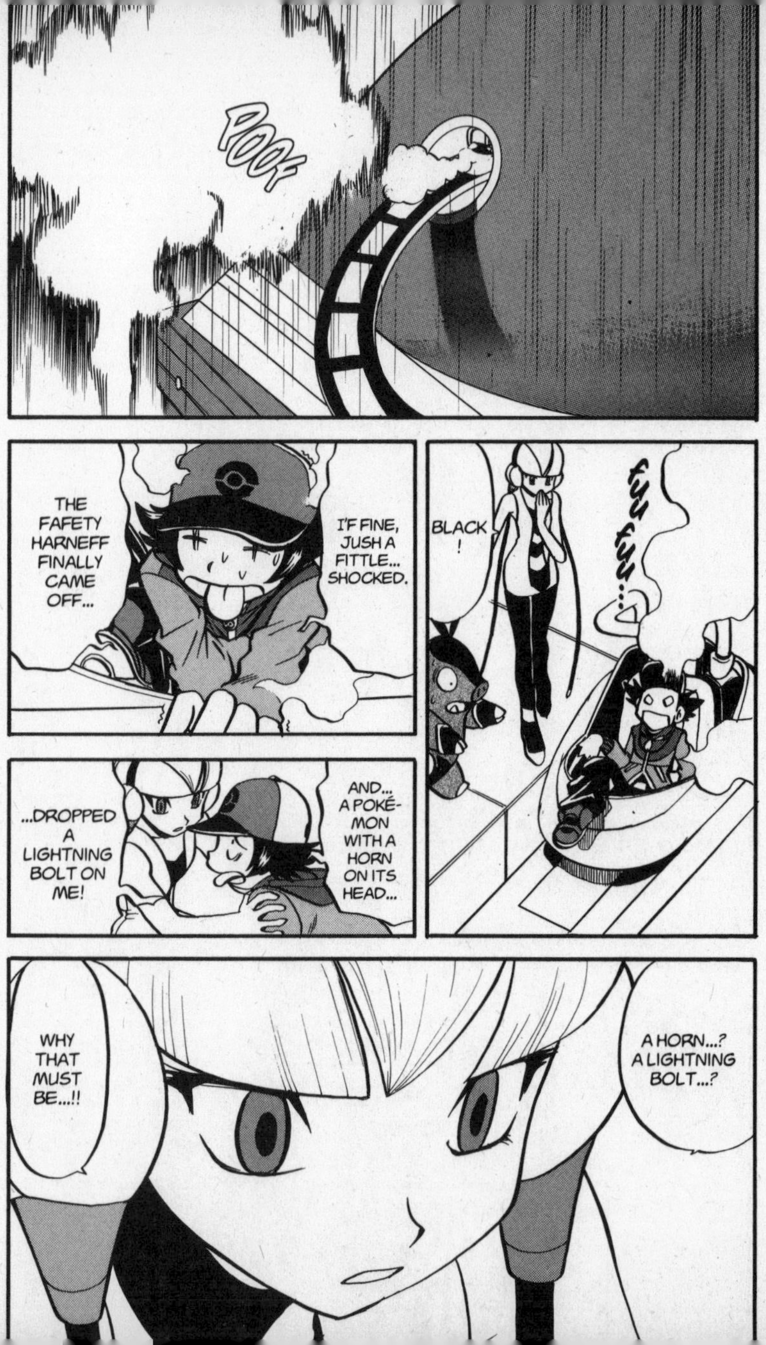
POOF
FUFUFU...
BLACK!
I'F FINE, JUSH A FITTLE... SHOCKED.
THE FAFETY HARNEFF FINALLY CAME OFF...
AND... A POKÉ-MON WITH A HORN ON ITS HEAD...
...DROPPED A LIGHTNING BOLT ON ME!
A HORN...? A LIGHTNING BOLT...?
WHY THAT MUST BE...!!

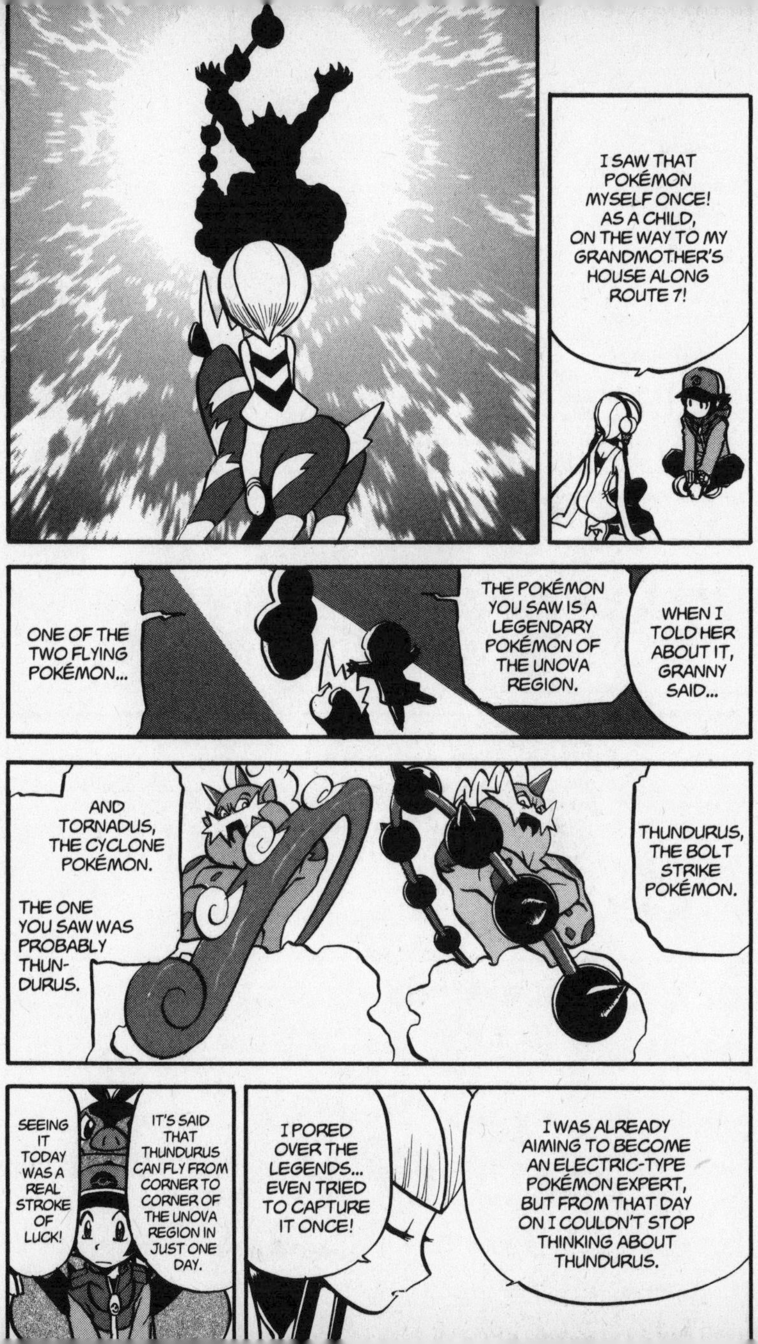
I SAW THAT POKÉMON MYSELF ONCE! AS A CHILD, ON THE WAY TO MY GRANDMOTHER'S HOUSE ALONG ROUTE 7!
WHEN I TOLD HER ABOUT IT, GRANNY SAID...
THE POKÉMON YOU SAW IS A LEGENDARY POKÉMON OF THE UNOVA REGION.
ONE OF THE TWO FLYING POKÉMON...
THUNDURUS, THE BOLT STRIKE POKÉMON.
AND TORNADUS, THE CYCLONE POKÉMON.
THE ONE YOU SAW WAS PROBABLY THUN-DURUS.
I WAS ALREADY AIMING TO BECOME AN ELECTRIC-TYPE POKÉMON EXPERT, BUT FROM THAT DAY ON I COULDN'T STOP THINKING ABOUT THUNDURUS.
I PORED OVER THE LEGENDS... EVEN TRIED TO CAPTURE IT ONCE!
IT'S SAID THAT THUNDURUS CAN FLY FROM CORNER TO CORNER OF THE UNOVA REGION IN JUST ONE DAY.
SEEING IT TODAY WAS A REAL STROKE OF LUCK!

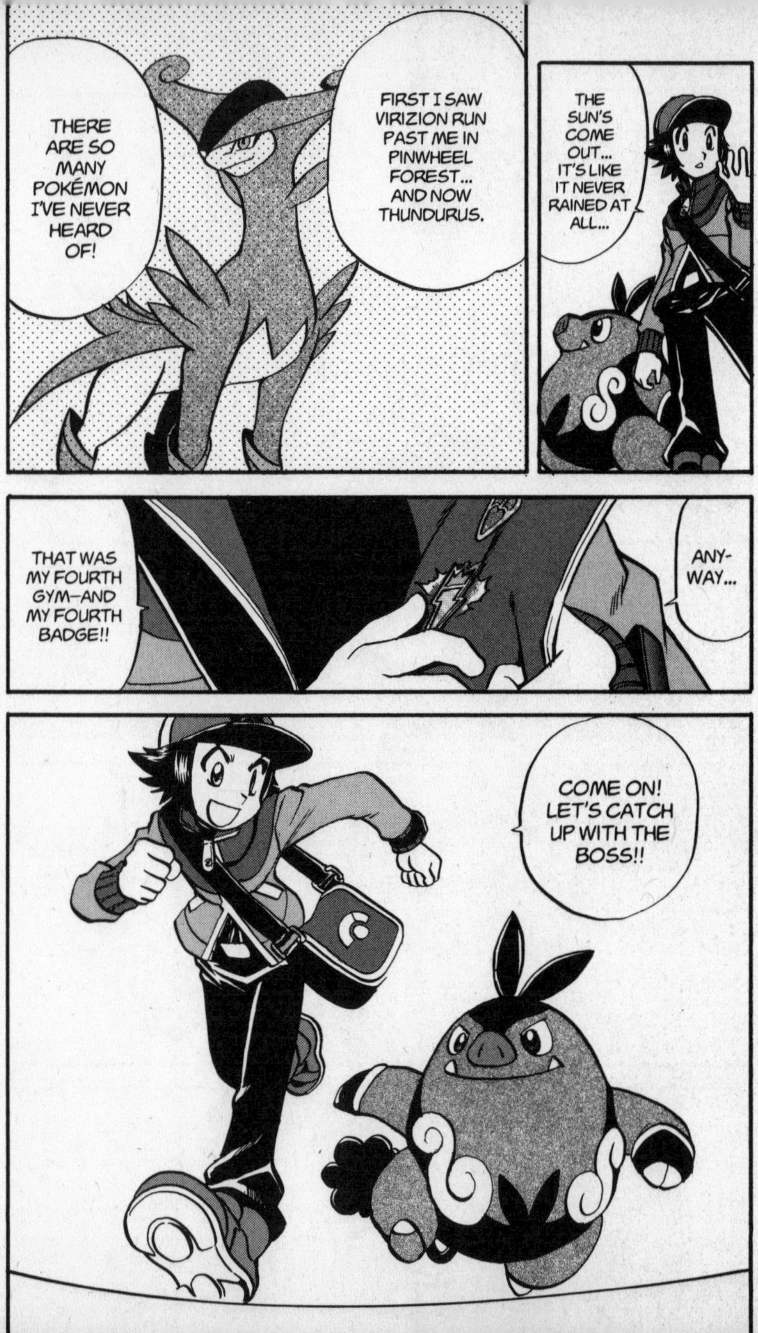
THERE ARE SO MANY POKÉMON I'VE NEVER HEARD OF!
FIRST I SAW VIRIZION RUN PAST ME IN PINWHEEL FOREST... AND NOW THUNDURUS.
THE SUN'S COME OUT... IT'S LIKE IT NEVER RAINED AT ALL...
THAT WAS MY FOURTH GYM—AND MY FOURTH BADGE!!
ANY-WAY...
COME ON! LET'S CATCH UP WITH THE BOSS!!

More Adventures COMING SOON...

White's beloved Pokémon and star performer Gigi abandons her for another Trainer! White receives his battle-trained Servine in exchange. But will White ever overcome her fears and learn to battle with her Pokémon?

VOL. 8 AVAILABLE JULY 2012!